Paralyzed Joy

Michelle Bader

Dedication

This book is dedicated to my husband Luke in heaven. You fought until the very last moment to be with your family. I know this was not the life we planned when we said "I do" nearly seventeen years ago, but the impact we have had is far greater than we could ever fathom. I know you have now received your miracle and you are healthy and whole and running with Jesus in heaven. Thank you for loving me for all these years. I will love you always and forever!

 Michelle

James 1:2-4 NIV

2 Consider it pure joy, my brothers and sisters, whenever you face trials of many kinds, 3 because you know that the testing of your faith produces perseverance. 4 Let perseverance finish its work so that you may be mature and complete, not lacking anything.

Introduction

*M*egan Montgomery has been given the rare privilege of seeing two different versions of how her life will playout. She gets to experience both lives and decide which one to return to. In one life her husband goes through extreme physical turmoil and in the other life her husband is perfectly healthy. She also visits heaven and learns valuable lessons while there that will help her make her final decision.

Chapter 1

"Daddy, dance with me," I said as I pulled on the arm of my father. "Okay Sunshine, anything for you," my dad said as he stood up out of his chair, reached for my hand and walked to the dance floor.

Well, it wasn't exactly a dance floor since we were in the gymnasium in our church, but to me it was the fanciest ball and we were the guests of honor. My pink sparkly dress shimmered as I walked. As the music played, I looked up into my daddy's eyes and in that moment, in my nine years of life I had never felt safer and more loved.

My daddy had a way of making me feel like nothing in the world could ever hurt me. He was my hero and that moment at the Father/Daughter Ball he was my king and I was his queen. My mother had helped me get ready for my special night out. She had curled my hair and listened to me as I talked of how excited I was for the night that I looked forward to more than any other night, even more than Christmas.

Going to the annual dance with my father was the highlight of my year. We always started the night out with him knocking on my bedroom door as he greeted me with a bouquet of flowers. He told me he was trying to show me how a real man should act on a date. During the dance he would awkwardly mingle with other dads which to me was a sign of how much he loved me. My dad was a quiet man who kept to himself, so I knew when he socialized with others it was way out of his comfort zone. Every year we would dance for hours as I kept asking him to dance with me song after song. We would dip strawberries and marshmallows in fancy chocolate fondue and eat until

2

we felt sick. For one night a year, I had my daddy's unwavering attention. Sure, I had his attention every day, but it was split with my two brothers and my mom. He did his best to make us all feel important, but this was the night I felt the most important.

As we swayed to the song *Butterfly Kisses,* I laid my head on his chest and heard the sound of his steady heartbeat. I closed my eyes and soaked in the moment. With my daddy's arms wrapped around me, I knew what it felt like to be loved. I knew what it meant to be treated like a queen. In that moment he set my standards high for any man who would ever take me out on a date. Little did I know that night would be the last of my special dances with my father.

***

"Daddy no, Daddy please don't go," I quivered in between sobs. My 10-year-old self could not comprehend the concept of death, so final, so cruel.

"My sunshine," my dad whispered in between gasps of air.
"I love you, always and forever." I strained to hear what my father was saying, clinging to every syllable as if it were the very air I was breathing.

"I love you too, Daddy," I said as I stared at the shell of the man I knew as my father. His body was just a shadow of the man I had known my whole life. Just a shell of the strong hands that held my own, just a shell of the feet I used to step on while he would dance with me and I would feel as though I was floating.

"Sunshine, you're special" he whispered as I responded the way I had for as long as I could remember.

"Daddy, you're specialer." and with those parting words, he was gone.

12 Years Later

I saw my reflection in the wooden full-length mirror in front of me. I turned my head from side to side, and my heart began to beat faster and faster as I looked at my beautiful white wedding dress. A sparkling tiara was upon my head, and light brown curls cascaded down my back. I stopped and stared at the image looking back at me, my green eyes piercing into my very soul.

I looked around the room and saw the people I loved most in the world surrounding me. My best friend was behind me adjusting my dress. She looked up and I could see tears brimming in her pale blue eyes. Sarah and I had been friends since we were five and she knew me better than any person on the earth. She had been there for me through the tears and heartaches and now joined me in the joys and celebrations of getting married.

"Megs I can't believe this day is here!" Sarah said enthusiastically as she adjusted my tiara.

"I know! It seems like just yesterday we were five years old pretending we were brides and here we are seventeen years later watching our dress-up play come to life!" I exclaimed.

My thoughts wandered to the man I was about to marry, the man I had dreamed of since I saw Cinderella and knew I wanted my own Prince Charming. Ryan Montgomery. My Ryan Montgomery. The thing I wanted most in life was to get married and have a family. When I met Ryan, I knew he was the one for me. Ryan had every quality I had ever wanted in a man. He also had everything I never knew I wanted. We were opposites in so many ways. Ryan was strong and stable and had a plan for every area of his life. I was fun and free and liked to go wherever the wind would take me. Ryan brought out the best in me and challenged me every day.

Although we were opposites in many ways, there was one major thing

that was important to us both: our relationships with God. Ryan exuded

faith. It seemed to come pouring out of him in every detail of his life.

We had both recently graduated college, and he had just started

working at Woodson's Law Firm. He was thriving in his new career

and seemed ready to take on the world. He was a light to all those

around him. His quiet but consistent faith was what drew others,

including myself to him.

I had chosen business as my major. I wasn't sure what I would do with

it as I hadn't yet landed a job. Ryan and I had long, deep talks about the

future. We dreamed of kids and vacations and growing old together.

Although I was excited about the possibilities for my new career, all I

really wanted to do was become a mom and stay home and take care of

my kids. Ryan had told me repeatedly how he supported my desire to

stay home and because of his new job, we would have the money to

allow that to be a reality. I was so thankful I would not have to work

and leave my kids. I had friends who wanted that, but for me, I just

wanted to be home and fulfill one of my lifelong dreams.

"Honey, you look beautiful," my mom's voice snapped me back to the

reality of my wedding day.

6

"Thank you, mom, don't cry, you will ruin your make-up," I said as I gazed at the woman who had played the largest role in helping me become the twenty-two-year-old young woman that was about to walk down the aisle.

My mom had not had it easy, and she had raised me as a single mom for most of my life, since my father had died when I was ten years old. I still carried the scars and weight of it and often wondered what life would be like if cancer had not taken him from me. What would it be like to have him walk me down the aisle? What would he say to me? One thing I knew for sure is that he would have loved Ryan. They would have gotten along amazingly well. I could picture my dad putting his arm around Ryan saying "Take care of my sunshine. Never let her light be dimmed." The images in my mind were a mixture of sweetness and sadness. "I love you Dad," I whispered under my breath.

I turned my thoughts back to my mother. She was everything I ever wanted to be. Adversity had sat at her door for as long as I could remember, but she never gave into its peril.

"Mom, I think I am ready," I said as I turned to look at her. I looked around the room and felt so much love. In addition to Sarah, I had six of my closest friends and my soon to be sister-in-law, Charlie. My friends included girls I had met in elementary school, high school, and college. There was not a clearer representation of who I was than the collective memories I had with these women; they knew what made me who I was. From Claire who shared lunches with me in kindergarten, to Lisa who met Ryan in college on the same night as me and everywhere in between, these women knew the real me. The me that was often hidden from those around me.

"Megan you look so beautiful," Claire said.

"Beautiful doesn't even begin to describe how amazing you look," Lisa added. I twirled one last time in front of the mirror. I had never in my life felt so much like a princess. *How did I get so lucky? Thank you, God, for this moment, for these friends and family and for my Ryan that I get to marry today!*

I began walking towards the door and towards my new future as Mrs. Megan Montgomery.

"I now pronounce you Mr. and Mrs. Ryan Montgomery."

With Ryan's hand in mine, we looked at each other with indescribable joy and began walking out of the church where we had just gotten married. "We did it, Baby!" Ryan exclaimed as he picked me up off of my feet and I shrieked in delight.

"I can't believe I'm your wife!" I said as I leaned up, looked into Ryan's deep brown eyes, and kissed him.

The rest of the evening came and went in a blur as we talked to our nearly three-hundred guests and danced the night away. I soon settled into the new normal of being Ryan's wife.

Chapter 2

Just a few months after we were married, I noticed something was off in my body. It seemed my stomach was upset constantly. I had always been healthy, so I found this feeling odd. *What if I am pregnant?* With that thought, I headed to the grocery store as fast as my VW bug could get me there. Walking from aisle to aisle I found what I was looking for, a pregnancy test. With my heart beating uncontrollably I purchased the test and headed to the restroom in the grocery store.

There is no way I can wait another moment, I thought. Carefully I read all the instructions, performed the test, and waited anxiously for the results. Slowly, I saw two pink lines beginning to appear on the thin white stick. As I watched, the pink lines grew brighter in intensity. I stared in shock and felt tears flowing down my face, tears of joy, tears for a life just beginning. I could hardly wait to tell Ryan! When Ryan returned home from work, I greeted him with a hug "What is it, my bride?"

"We are having a baby!" I said excitedly. Ryan's eyes filled with tears as he stared at me intently. To say he was excited was an understatement. Months went by and the day I had been waiting for finally arrived.

"Ryan, I can't believe today we find out if we are having a boy or a girl!" I exclaimed as I squeezed his strong hand in the waiting room of our doctor's office.

Ryan's eyes met my own, and he smiled. I could read his excitement by the way his eyes sparkled, and his dimples began to show.

I had wanted to be a mom for as long as I could remember. Sure, I had my own ambitions and goals too, but nothing appealed to me as much as bringing a new life into the world.

Laying on the crinkly paper in the exam room, I anticipated the news of our baby. Cold gel covered my enlarged stomach, and the ultrasound tech began to move her wand around. Instantly I saw an image on the screen that started to come into focus. The profile of my baby came into view. I could not believe my eyes. This beautiful human was my baby, part Ryan and part me. The miracle I saw took my breath away.

11

"Are you ready to find out what you are having?" the technician's voice said quickly.

"Yes," Ryan and I said in unison. Our eyes stared intently at the screen as unrecognizable images appeared. To me what was a blur, revealed to the trained technician's eyes the sex of our baby.

"It's a girl."

I squeezed Ryan's hand and gasped in delight.

"Our baby girl, our baby Madelyn, our little Maddy," I said as I smiled, already feeling more love for this baby girl than I knew possible. Just saying her name out loud made her more real and solidified the fact that the growing child inside of me would soon join our family. Each move she made brought me closer to the reality of holding my dream.

I gazed over at Ryan and saw his eyes beginning to brim with tears. Although I knew he was secretly disappointed that his baseball glove and sports paraphernalia would go untouched for the time being, I knew his heart was being melted at the thought of a baby girl to call him Daddy.

Since Ryan had come straight from work, we drove in separate cars. Hand in hand we walked to the parking lot both lost in thoughts and dreams for the exciting future with our baby Maddy. Stopping at my bright yellow Volkswagen Beetle, I said, "It's time to think about upgrading to a family car."

"But please not a minivan," he said quickly. We both laughed as we had talked many times about never wanting to turn into a minivan family.

Ryan glanced down at his watch, "I have to go, Baby, I have a huge case I need to get back to."

I looked up into his deep brown eyes, and with a quick kiss on the lips, he was gone.

As I watched my husband walk away my heart had never felt fuller. "You have a great Daddy," I said as I rubbed my protruding stomach. As if Maddy could understand me she quickly kicked me twice. Laughter escaped me and tears of joy fell from my eyes.

Maddy...my baby Maddy. I wonder who she will look like? Will she have blue eyes or brown? Light hair or dark? Would she have her

Daddy's unmistakable dimples? My whole fifteen-minute drive home I ran countless questions through my head.

I arrived home, and as I was walking through the door, I heard the familiar ring of my cell phone.

Digging through my purse, I finally reached it. An unknown number appeared across the screen. "Telemarketers," I mumbled under my breath. Entering my house, the phone began to ring again. Again, I sent it to voicemail. I was in the habit of ignoring unknown numbers. A third time, my phone rang. "Okay, okay, I'll answer!" I said annoyed.

"Hello," I answered hesitantly.

"Is this Megan Montgomery?"

"Yes," I said still guarding myself against the sale I was sure was about to be pushed.

"Mrs. Montgomery, there has been an accident."

In an instant, I felt my heart drop to the floor. I could feel myself getting pale, and my head began to get fuzzy.

"What, who?" I practically screamed.

"Your husband Ryan, was in a car accident and is being life-flighted to Emanuel hospital, please come to the emergency room quickly" she explained.

The phone felt like it weighed a million pounds as it dropped out of my hand. Still in shock, I ran back to my car without even remembering to lock the front door of the house.

"No...no...no...no" I yelled as warm tears ran down my face. "Not my Ryan, not my Ryan." With one hand on the wheel and one hand on my stomach, I said, "Daddy is going to be okay Maddy, Daddy is going to be okay." Feeling as though I was in a nightmare, I drove the short three miles to the hospital as if on autopilot.

Heart pounding and mind spinning I got out of my car as fast as I could manage. My eyes were scanning the signs above, and I quickly found the sign with bold red letters marked Emergency Room. The sliding doors opened, and I rushed to the counter oblivious of the crowd of people I cut in front of. When the receptionist looked at me, I knew she had seen this frantic look from a loved one too many times to count.

"Where is my husband?" my voice nearly screamed, "Ryan Montgomery, please he has been in an accident."

"Ma'am, I need you to calm down, let me look up where he is." As the seconds ticked by it felt like an eternity to me as she clicked through pages on her computer screen.

"Mrs. Montgomery, he is in surgery," the woman explained. You need to wait in the waiting room, and the doctor will come to see you when he is out of surgery."

"Wait, can you tell me anything?" I pleaded.

"I'm sorry, I really can't," she replied without a hint of sensitivity in her voice. *What am I going to do?* I fell to my knees, too weak to stand. I decided it was time to call my mom.

While I waited for my mom to pick up the phone, I felt Maddy kick again. "It's okay Maddy; Daddy is going to be okay," I said. *Was I speaking to her or to myself?* My thoughts were interrupted when my mom said, "Hi, Megan" in her usual upbeat tone.

"Mom," I cried as tears cascaded down my face and I tried to find words. "It's Ryan; he has been in an accident."

"What happened?" she asked.

"I don't know, they won't tell me, I am at Emanuel Hospital" I answered.

"I'm on my way," my mom replied without hesitation.

I looked around the large waiting room and saw people in all directions. Mothers were holding their injured children and people of all ages were waiting their turn to be seen. As Maddy continued to kick, my mind continued to spin. All I knew was that my Ryan had been in a terrible car accident and was in surgery, that was it. No details, just me left to my imagination and thoughts of the worst possible scenarios. Within minutes I saw my mom running towards me.

"Megan," she said softly as she welcomed me into her warm embrace. More tears began to fall as I lost all control of my body and began to collapse.

"Megan, where is Ryan now?" she asked.

"Surgery, mom, I don't even know what kind of surgery!"

"Okay, you should sit down, and I will see what I can find out."

As I watched my mom walk away, I realized how difficult visiting this place must be for her. This was the place where my father had spent countless nights getting chemo. The place where he had blood transfusions, painful procedures and where he eventually took his last breath.

"Daddy," I whispered as the mere thought of him brought such a mixture of pain and happiness.

Within minutes my mom returned. "Megan we can go wait in a different area. I think I found someone who can tell us more." She helped me up, and we made our way through the maze of hallways that led us to a smaller, quieter waiting room. A few minutes later I saw a woman in scrubs approaching us.

"Mrs. Montgomery?" the woman asked with a kind smile on her face. "Yes?"

"Hi, I'm Jackie, the nurse assigned to your husband. I wanted to come out and talk to you, so you have some idea about what is happening to

18

him. As you know, he is in surgery. He has internal bleeding in his brain. The surgery we are performing right now is called a decompression surgery; we are doing this to remove pressure on his brain and remove any pools of blood."

"Okay," I replied, still not comprehending the words being said to me. She continued, "In addition to the internal bleeding we believe he may have broken his neck. After surgery, we will be performing X-rays and scans. As soon as the surgeon is out of surgery, he will come to talk to you."

I felt a single warm tear fall from my eye, as I watched her walk away. Minutes dragged into hours, and I saw a man in scrubs walking towards me.

"Mrs. Montgomery?" he asked.

"Yes?"

"I am Dr. Watson; I just finished surgery on your husband. I wanted to tell you the good news, the decompression surgery was a success, and we have removed all the pools of blood. The not so good news is that his spinal cord was severed. I am so sorry to tell you that when the semi-truck hit your husband's car, it broke his neck."

"No, please no!" I exclaimed.

Dr. Watson continued, "Mrs. Montgomery, we are hoping that your husband will make a full recovery from the brain injury, but unfortunately, it looks like he may be permanently paralyzed."

My world went dark. Blackness enveloped me. Pictures tried to form in front of my eyes, but I could not see them. Words were being spoken, but I could not hear them. I knew I must be in some kind of nightmare. *Wake up Megan, wake up*! I screamed silently. As the darkness subsided, I tried to form words.

"C-can you say that again?" I stammered. "Yes, Mrs. Montgomery, your husband may be permanently paralyzed."

And with that, I knew that my worst nightmare was, in fact, a reality.

Chapter 3

I began the long walk to the hospital room where they would soon bring Ryan. The echo of the hallway reminded me again of where I was. Growing up I spent a lot of time in the sterile hospital environment. I remember before my father's death that hospitals used to be a place full of adventure. My brothers and I would explore and feast on the vending machine snacks we found on various floors. Hospitals were part of my normal life. All of that changed the day I said goodbye to my father. Hospitals became a place of death, the place that took my father from me; they no longer held any adventure or fun.

Here I was again, but this time I would not let death's icy grip touch me. I would not lose another person to this place. Ryan might be paralyzed, but he wasn't dead. Thinking of that brought Ryan's accident into perspective. At least he wasn't killed instantly in what could have easily been a deadly tragedy

My heart quickened as I tried to imagine how Ryan would react when he learned he was paralyzed. *Did he already know? What would he say to me? Would he cry?* Anticipation overtook my emotions as I stopped outside of room 727.

"Do you want me to go with you or wait outside?" my mom asked peering into the room.

"I think I should go alone at first," I replied quickly.

Cautiously I put one lead foot in front of the other and walked towards my husband. As I got closer to him, I could see metal rods going from his neck to his head and attaching to a metal circular rod that was around his head, known as a halo brace. I knew that the halo was there to help secure and aid in the healing of his neck and spinal cord. I desperately wanted to look away, the pain of the reality of the image in front of me was almost too much to bear.

Ryan's eyes were closed, and his face tightened as if he was in pain. His lifeless body was tucked under a myriad of blankets, and all that was visible was his robotic looking head and neck.

I began to doubt my ability to take another step forward and face my husband. *I can do all things through Christ who strengthens me,* the words I had memorized so many years ago came back to me in an instant, the exact moment that I needed them the most. Suddenly filled with an infusion of strength I approached Ryan.

"Hi, Baby," I said softly placing my hand upon Ryan's shoulder. *Could he even feel that?* I wondered. Ryan did not move. His eyes remained shut, and his face remained tight.

I kept my hand on his shoulder, not knowing what to do next. *God help us.* I prayed silently, *Please God*!

"Mom, you can come in now," I said to my mother who was just outside of the door to Ryan's room. I watched as my mom looked in Ryan's direction. She slowly made her way over to the hospital bed. The worried look in her eyes told me that not only was she living the pain of seeing Ryan like this, but also reliving the memories of my father and his time spent in hospitals as well. I hated that she had to be back here in the hospital, to feel the pain once again.

"Hey Ryan, we are praying for you," my mom said as she gently touched his shoulder.

Again, Ryan did not move. He remained in his unmoving, lifeless state. Occasionally, he would tense up as if in pain or look as though he was going to wake up. Looking at my husband of less than a year I faced an even more earth-shattering reality...he may wake up and never remember me. He may have forgotten me, our first kiss, our dreams, and even our unborn baby Maddy.

As the day wore on, we were visited by many friends and family. Each time one entered there was always an awkward silence and pause as they seemed to be deciding on the appropriate thing to say. I understood their difficulty. I got it. What do you say to the pregnant, newlywed wife of an unconscious, paralyzed man with possible amnesia?

"Megan," my mom interrupted my thoughts "You need to eat."

Eating was the last thing I was thinking of. I looked at my husband again, "Mom, how can I eat when he is like this?!" I could no longer hold back the waterfalls that now escaped my eyes. All braveness I had tried to exude throughout the day melted away, and I was left with the rawness of the reality before me.

"Come here Megan," my mom said as she opened her arms and invited me to sit on her lap. Letting time disappear, I walked to my mother and allowed all the physical and emotional weight I had been carrying to dissipate on to her body. As if I was still a young child, I lost my ability

24

to contain my emotions and I let out the pain I had been trying to stifle all day. With wails from a hidden place too deep to see, I proceeded to let the tears and pain out.

"It's okay my girl, it's okay," my mom rocked me back and forth as if we were suddenly transported back twenty years.

"God, please help my baby girl," my mom began to pray.

"Please give her strength, comfort, and peace. We pray for healing for Ryan. We pray that you heal his body, mind, and spirit. We pray that he has his full memory when he wakes up, and we pray he regains full functionality of his entire body." I silently agreed with her prayer and laid my head upon her chest. The beating of her heart gave me comfort the way it had so many times in the past. The way it did on the countless nights when I cried for my dad's cancer to go away, the nights that I prayed that my dad would be healed. The way I cried as I watched other girls play with their dads and the way I cried just months before when my dad wasn't there to walk me down the aisle.

Growing up with a sick father who eventually died left me with so many questions. I used to struggle with why God had never healed my dad. I didn't understand how a good and loving God would take the person more precious than anyone on the earth away from me. I wrestled with these questions for years, but as I questioned, my faith deepened. Each question brought me closer to the loving arms of my heavenly father. Each question became an opportunity for Him in all his loving kindness and grace to show me his love.

Through my questioning, I began to understand that I would never understand it all. I realized that God did not cause my father to die, nor did he create the sickness. I began to comprehend through the pain that God knows so much more than I ever could. I learned that if God allowed it, I could accept it. Through the eventual acceptance of losing my father, I began to experience a more profound faith and trust than I would have ever had without the pain. In the twelve years since his death, I had come to embrace that God has a plan more significant than I could comprehend and I learned to rest entirely in that fact.

Yet here I was again. With a new wound so deep, it threatened to undo years of trust and faith. In an instant, the uncertainties tried to take over my mind. *No, I will not go backwards! I know who my God is and He has a plan, He is for me and not against me and I will not waiver in my faith just because I can't see how to get past this mountain staring me down.* Suddenly my resolve and confidence in the one who carried me through countless times of doubt was back. I shuddered at the thought of how close I came to losing my faith.

With the sound of my mom's heartbeat in my ear and the hope of my God in my heart, I resolved to trust God with my unknown future and be the best wife and advocate possible, with every fiber of my being for Ryan's recovery.

Chapter 4

A short time after breaking down on my mom's lap I found the energy to eat. I knew that despite how I was feeling Maddy needed the nourishment food would provide for her. Having Maddy living inside of me inspired me to keep going. The light crept through the window inside of room 727. A room that I knew we would need to get used to being our home for the duration of Ryan's recovery.

A little while later I noticed Ryan's fingers beginning to twitch. His toes also began to move, I could see his foot beginning to jerk.

"God please let him wake up," I whispered as I stared at Ryan.

"Baby, I am here, I'm here," I said as I stroked his face hoping and praying that this, in fact, would be the moment my husband would come back to me.

One brown eye opened and then another. Wide-eyed Ryan began peering from left to right. His eyes scanned the room trying to make sense of his surroundings. "Where am I?"

"Ryan, you are in the hospital, you were in an accident."

In a panic, he shouted, "Why can't I move my legs, why can't I move my arms?" I observed him struggling in what appeared to be an effort to move. Holding back tears I tried to calmly explain.

"Ryan, when the semi-truck hit you the impact was so extreme that your spinal cord was severed. I'm sorry, but it looks like you may never walk again" I watched his panic turn into despair. I could read through his eyes and into his soul as though I could feel his very being crumble under the news.

Laying a hand of comfort on his shoulder I began to pray. "Jesus we come to you now, scared and shocked, we do not know what the future holds, we pray for a full recovery." struggling to get out the words I let my silent tears fall from my face.

"Megan," Ryan said as his eyes remained wide in disbelief. Consumed with seeing him struggle I suddenly remembered that memory loss had been a risk. *Thank you God*, that he remembers me I quickly and silently prayed. I don't think I could stand to see him not remembering me!

"Megan, why is this happening? Why me?" Ryan shouted. There were no sufficient words I could say to him to ease his pain. No magic words to make things better. All I could do was sit there, by his side, holding his lifeless hand and praying for a miracle.

Ryan's eyes seemed to still be struggling to make sense of his new reality. I knew this was just the beginning of a long road to recovery. My dreams of traveling and taking long walks later in life were fading with every thought of my husband's current state. With news of Ryan being awake, the doctor had been sent for. A tall, lanky man with wire-rimmed glasses and a clipboard entered the room, though he was looking our way there seemed to be no emotion on his face.

"Ryan, I am so glad you are awake, are you aware of what is going on?" he said as he stepped closer to us.

"Yes, my wife told me. I know about the accident and I know I most likely will be paralyzed forever," Ryan replied as he fought to hold back the tears I could see brimming in his eyes.

Dr. Greenwood walked closer and began examining Ryan. He inspected the halo to make sure it was in the correct position.

"How long will I have to wear this?" Ryan said and I knew he was referring to the metal encasement around his head.

"It depends on a lot of unknown factors. We will take it one day at a time. Our first goal is to get you out of the hospital and into a rehabilitation center, they have more resources and programs for you there."

After a few more minutes and a lot more questions, we were left alone again in the sterile hospital room. I had no idea how Ryan would have the physical strength to recover and even more, I had no idea if I would have the emotional and mental strength it would take to continue on the road that now appeared to be our future. The road that included, doctors, nurses, iv's catheters, bedpans, fluorescent lights, no sleep, and strength beyond our own human capacity.

Though my heart was breaking I tried to stuff the pain deep inside of me. I knew my role was now to be the strong one in the situation. I understood I was suddenly thrown into the role I never desired in order to keep things together.

I was used to being the emotional one. Ryan often told me I was like the stock market. My moods were up and down and sometimes hard to predict. I must now put my own wants and desires away and focus solely on helping Ryan recover.

Looking at my husband of less than a year my mind filled with endless questions. *What would his recovery look like? Would he make a full recovery? What would he do for a job? Would Maddy ever see her father walk? Would he ever play with her? Would she know the joy of dancing and being swirled around by him? Would we ever have any more kids?*

31

My thoughts were interrupted by words I had heard more times than I can count.

"Remember I know the plans for your life, I am here to prosper you and not harm you" Though I had heard these words for as long as I could remember, they suddenly took on a deeper meaning. *God, how in the world could this be a plan to prosper me or my Ryan? How could this be a good plan for Maddy? What in the world are you doing! I hate the pain of this moment; can you please help us?*

My eyes returned to my husband. "What are you thinking?" I asked

"I'm thinking about our Maddy. I'm thinking about how she will never know me as whole and complete. I…" Ryan's voice began to crack as I could see he was fighting the tears that were trying to make their way down his face.

"I can't do this Megan. I can't go on like this. I wish I would have died in the accident" His chest began to heave uncontrollably as he struggled to catch his breath. Over and over he reached for air that seemed to be invisibly gone. I stroked his hand as my own tears fell upon his head.

"It's okay my love, it's okay" I repeated over and over trying to convince myself more than just him.

"I am so glad you didn't die, Maddy and I need you. She needs her daddy. Part of my growing up happened without a father and I don't want that for her. You are stronger than you think, and I know we will get through this. Also, as we say all the time, Montgomery's don't give up!" His face began to soften as I heard a small laugh escape from his tense body.

I resolved at that moment that I needed and would continue to put on a strong face in front of him. My husband had nearly died, and I needed to be as strong for him as I could as he began the long journey of recovering. Although I knew he would most likely never fully recover, I knew my job was to be there in the good days and bad days. I would not leave his side even on the darkest nights. I was chosen by God for this moment, I was chosen since before I was born to be Ryan's wife. I was chosen because God knew I could stand by Ryan's side and endure the waves of grief and pain that were sure to come.

Chapter 5

When Ryan awoke, he again looked confused. I could see his senses trying to take in his current surroundings. He was observing the bright lights shining down, the beeping of machines, and the hard bed he was lying on. As his eyes looked into my own, I could feel my heart breaking once again.

"Mrs. Montgomery" I heard the soft voice of a nurse say as she approached Ryan's bed.

"Yes," I replied hesitantly- guarding my emotions as I felt if one more thing went wrong it would be the rock cascading into my frozen lake and breaking the layer of ice covering my inner being.

"It is time for your husband to try to move, would you like to be part of the process?"

"Of course," I replied robotically.

'Ryan, can you feel this?" the nurse said as she placed her hand upon his shoulder.

"No" he quickly replied.

"What about this?" she said as she placed her hand upon his bare toes. A smile spread wide across his face as he almost shouted: "Yes, I think I can!" What a relief! If he could feel his toes there might still be hope for him.

"Thank you, God," I whispered under my breath. Motioning to me the nurse said, "Please touch his face." As if it was the first time for my hands to touch his face, I gently put my hand on his cheek. Looking into Ryan's deep brown eyes I said "Do you feel this?'

Tears welled up in his eyes It feels so good to have you touch my face and know I can always feel that gentle stroke when I need comfort Visions of my strong husband carrying our baby home from the hospital began to fade. The thought of him throwing a baseball or tossing a football around began to sink. I felt as if I was on a sinking boat with no way to get the water out. One wave after another crashed over me as I gasped for breath and felt the water cascade over my mouth and body. There was no way out. This was my new reality. The dreams of my future were shattered. life as I knew it had changed. My sadness turned to anger in an instant. "Why God, why!" I screamed silently.

"*Just end it all, this is too much pain*" I heard the words in my mind so clearly as if they were being spoken through a megaphone. Thoughts of ending the pain gave me relief for a minute until I thought of the pain that would also affect those, I loved the most. In addition, I had another life living in me who counted on me for her every need. Where did that thought come from? I had never thought of that ever in my life, but the voice came so strong that I knew I didn't make it up. Suddenly I realized I was under attack. I remembered an important verse I had memorized years ago.

"*For our struggle is not against flesh and blood, but against the authorities against the powers of this dark world and against the spiritual forces of evil in the heavenly realms.* "
Ephesians 6:12 NIV

As my physical world was in a battle so was my spiritual world. Filling my mind louder than the previous megaphone I remembered that our struggles were not against people but against an unknown world that we couldn't see. With these words fresh in my mind I began to comprehend the immense battle I found myself in the middle of. This was not only a war on Ryan's body but a war on us spiritually, it would be a war to test what we believe and how we believe. Would we crumble under the pressure of the accident? Would we run to God to seek his comfort or strength? Would our faith be enough?

I sat down on the small chair next to Ryan's hospital bed and closed my eyes, then the unexplainable happened.

A bright light enveloped me and all I could see were flashes of light and at an intensity, I had never known. Thoughts and sounds seemed to whirl around me in all directions. When I opened my eyes I was in a field of bright yellow tulips.

A strange calm and peace seemed to permeate my being. I could just make out the sound of a brook babbling in the distance as I sat up and tried to take in my surroundings.

The intensity of the light grew stronger as it came closer, bringing with it an unexplainable feeling of peace. What my eyes saw my mind could not comprehend.

"Welcome Megan," a deep voice said.

"Where am I? What is happening?" I asked frantically, trying to make sense of my current reality.

"You are in heaven," replied the voice again. I heard the words, but they didn't make sense to my confused mind.

"Megan, you have been given a rare gift, you have been given the gift of another chance at life."

"How did I get here?" I spoke quickly.

"It is all part of the process" He replied.

"It is time for you to see another version of your life" and with that, my world started to spin again.

***

Suddenly I saw myself standing in front of the mirror twirling. It was my wedding day once again. Confused I looked at my friends and family surrounding me. Was I really going to do this whole day again?

The day once again continued as it had before. Although I had already lived this day, I felt the same emotions again. After the wedding day, things continued exactly the same as I had experienced before.

October 8th started the way the other October 8th had started. Ryan and I once again had our ultrasound and once again found out that we would be having a baby girl. Our little baby Maddy. As we said goodbye in the parking lot, my mind was uneasy remembering what had happened before on this day. I lingered longer as we said goodbye, not wanting to leave his arms.

"Baby, what is wrong, why are you acting so funny?" Ryan said as we walked to our cars.

Thinking it would be the last time I would see him walk I soaked in every second of having an able-bodied husband.

"I just love you so much." I managed to say while holding back tears.

" I love you too, but you have to let go, I have to get back to work if you want me to continue to have a job to provide for you and Maddy," He said with a smile and a twinkle in his eyes. Reluctantly I let go. My mind spun into action. Maybe I could prevent the accident from happening!

"Ryan, I will take you back to work"
"That doesn't make sense, please just let me go, I love you and I will see you tonight" and with that, he was off.

Tears fell quickly down my face as I knew what was about to happen, or so I thought.
Slowly and reluctantly I drove the short drive home dreading the call that I knew was about to happen,

As I pulled into our driveway I looked down at my phone. I braced myself for the call that would change our lives. The minutes slowly passed and there was no call. I decided to call Ryan myself. As the phone rang twice my heart began to pound faster. With each missed ring my fears grew stronger. After four rings it went to voicemail. I turned back to my car and knew what I needed to do.

Quickly I drove the few short miles to Ryan's work. If he wouldn't answer I would have to go lay eyes on him and see what was happening. I parked the car, skipping the elevator and running up the stairs. Heart pounding, I opened the door to the 5th floor and quickly made my way to the door marked Woodson's Law Firm.

"Is Ryan here?" I blurted out to the receptionist between gasps of air.

"Yes, are you okay?" she replied seeing the panic in my face and the fear in my eyes. I continued running as I made my way to the office marked "Ryan L. Montgomery" I burst open the door to find Ryan on the phone. Seeing the fear in my eyes he quickly hung up the phone.

"Baby what is it?'" Ryan exclaimed as he ran to me. I burst into tears as he put his strong arms around me, and I melted in the warmth of his arms. The fear from the alternate day of his accident disappeared as I realized that this was another version of my life.

I liked this version. In this version, I felt safe and loved and my world wasn't crumbling. In this life, my husband was happy and whole. We had a new little life to look forward to with no signs of accidents in the future. In this life, my world had not been rocked and I could predict what the future would hold. There were no doctors and hospitals, nurses, or bedpans. There were no long nights in the hospital and my visions of Ryan playing with our future children were still intact.

There were no fears of how to survive financially and no wonders about if my husband would ever walk or bathe on his own.

"Thank you, God," I whispered under my breath. Thank you for giving me the version that I am sure is the reality I am meant to have. And with that, I took a deep breath and settled into my new reality.

Chapter 6

The days turned into weeks and weeks turned into months and I found myself thinking about the birth of Maddy with greater anticipation but also uneasiness. On one hand, I couldn't wait to hold her in my arms and feel the softness of her skin. On the other hand, even the birth process scared me. I had watched dozens of episodes of The Baby Story, but not one of them gave me any comfort after seeing the birth scenes. My body was no longer my own as every inch seemed to be taken up or used for the development of my baby, Madelyn Joy Montgomery.

Just saying her name out loud brought me to an emotional level I had never known. Until seeing her ultrasound pictures and hearing her heartbeat I had never known a love so deep. Sure, my love for Ryan was deep, but this was on a whole new level.

My pains increased hourly and my contractions started coming closer together. At last, I knew it was time. Ryan helped me into his truck as we drove the short few miles to the hospital. As I tried to muffle the pain I was having, Ryan reached over.

"How are you doing baby?"

"Okay, just get me there as quickly as possible." I gasped through another painful contraction. As we approached the hospital, images of my father appeared in my head. A wave of sadness washed over me *He should be here*, I thought. Near the end of my father's life, he was not the same man I had known as a younger child. His once vibrant smile had been darkened under the weight of his pain. As the tumors grew so did his anxiety. He struggled to remain in a place of peace as he knew that death awaited him.

Although he knew his death would lead to an eternal destination of glory, he struggled with the thoughts of leaving us behind. The intensely painful thought of leaving his wife and children on earth without him would sometimes spiral him into a dark period of depression. As a young child, I didn't understand the depths of his emotions. Each time he would cry or yell, my mom would tell us, it was not him speaking, but his pain and medicine.

Each time he said an unkind word to us my mom was always there to soften the blow and try to ease the pain by deflecting what he said because of the pain and medicine. I never realized how hard she worked to protect us from the pain, how she tirelessly fought for us and fought for peace in our home. When my dad was extremely unkind, she would always find an excuse for us to leave.

"Who feels like ice cream?" she would often say with a smile on her face as she tried to hide the tears in her eyes. As I felt my time fast approaching, to becoming a mom I began to comprehend more and more of what my mom had done for us in the most tumultuous of times.

The outside world never knew what a battlefield our world was at home. To the public, my mom always painted my father in the best light. To onlookers, he was a man at peace who pushed hard to be there for his family, and yes, he was but there was much more to the story. I remember wondering many times what it would be like to have a healthy dad. I can't count how many times I watched my friends with their dads and closed my eyes and imagined what it would be like to have a dad free from cancer, pain and ultimately death.

How would my life have been different? What would he be feeling on this day, the day he would become a grandpa? That's the thing about death, no matter how much time has passed, there is still a sting, sometimes intense and sometimes barely noticeable, but always there. Today the sting was intense as I felt a hole in the place where he should be.

In the hospital bed, hooked up to an epidural my pain subsided, and anticipation took over. I was about to have my Maddy, my own little sunshine. The pressure of the contractions increased, and I knew it was time to meet my baby. With Ryan on one side and my mother on the other, we welcomed Madelyn Joy Montgomery into the world. As she was laid on top of me, I looked into Ryan's eyes and for a moment the world felt complete and whole. Within a few seconds she let out a healthy cry and we laughed in unison.

"She has your lungs" I said, as I gazed at Ryan.

I was soon engulfed in a new world that included nursing and diaper changes. I was quickly getting the hang of both and settling into my new role as a mother. Driving home from the hospital looking between Ryan and Maddy I felt more complete than I ever had in my entire life. I had everything I ever dreamed of.

My Ryan, such a strong, handsome, healthy man, such a bright future ahead for him at the law firm. And now I had Maddy, I had finally become what I always dreamed of, being a mom to change the diapers, fold the laundry, attend PTA meetings, and bring snacks to soccer games.

"Thank you, God," I said aloud as I continued gazing at the two loves of my life. Life could not be more perfect.

45

I shut my eyes and breathed in deeply. Relaxation and peace overtook my entire body. Feeling as though I was in a deep sleep, I let my body relax. Opening my eyes, a moment later I found myself once again amidst a field of yellow tulips. Shocked I stood up and all I could see were flowers in every direction. The warmth of the sunshine permeated my entire being and I realized I must once again be in heaven.

Slowly turning in all directions, I began to see a shape in the distance. I couldn't yet make out what it was. As it got closer the shapeless form began to look like a man. Not yet able to make out his face I wondered what this man was doing in what appeared to be heaven when there was no one else around. As he walked closer, he began to look more familiar.

In an instant, I recognized his face. His face was the unmistakable face of my dad, but my dad from his younger healthier years. His dark brown eyes, olive complexion, and brown hair matched the picture that still adorned my mom's house when they were just dating.

"Daddy?" I said as I began running towards him. Arms wide open he picked me up as though I was a child again.

"My Sunshine" he said as he twirled me around. There were no words to describe the feeling of being reunited with the first man I ever loved. He put me down and I stared into his deep brown eyes.

"Daddy, I have missed you!" I exclaimed while observing his once again healthy body. Gone was any trace of sickness in his body. The frail man I knew upon his death was replaced by this vibrant youthful version I now saw before me. When he took his last breath on earth, I had tried to imagine this version of him. When I had watched his body deteriorate, I had found comfort in knowing he would soon have a new body. The man in front of me exuded health. The smile on his face was bigger and brighter than any smile I had ever seen. His face almost looked as though it was glowing.

"Oh Sunshine, your baby Maddy is so beautiful, I couldn't be more proud of you."

"You, you know about her?" I stared in disbelief.

"Yes, my Sunshine, I am able to share in the special moments, just like I was there when you married your Ryan. What a good man he is" he said with a twinkle in his eyes.

"You, you were there at my wedding?" I stammered.

"Yes, and all your beautiful moments along the way. I was so proud of you on both your high school and college graduation days."

This must be a dream I thought. My senses told me it was real, but the unending field of tulips and the presence of my father made me believe it wasn't.

"Sunshine, I understand you have been given a rare gift. I understand that you are getting to see two different versions of your life play out. One where your dear husband Ryan is paralyzed and one where he is not. How is it going so far?"

His question caught me off guard as the life with paralyzed Ryan seemed like a distant dream. One that I hadn't thought about in a long time. In fact, I often imagined that one never actually happened and it was, in fact, a nightmare.

"Oh Daddy, the one where he was paralyzed was so awful. So very awful. I hated seeing him in so much pain. He was so helpless and sad. Just when things were getting really bad, I had the chance to live everything again without him getting hurt. Daddy, this version is so much better. I get to experience life as I thought it would be. I get the dream husband and family I always wanted."

"That is great Sunshine. Tell me why this life is so much better?" he said with an inquisitive look on his face.

Thinking this was obvious, his question took me by surprise.

"Well, there is a lot less pain. I don't have to see my sweet husband suffer. My baby will know her daddy as healthy and well."

"I understand," my father said with his hand on his chin, something he always did when he was contemplating something.

"Sweetie, did you ever stop to think that maybe the pain is part of the plan to grow you and Ryan and even baby Maddy into who He wants you to become? I am not saying God caused this to happen, but all I am saying is that if God allowed it, you can accept it and know with certainty that God will use it and He will make beauty out of all of these ashes. God even goes so far as to ask us to consider it pure joy when we face trials, pure joy baby girl. This was a concept I wish that I would have understood on earth. You know why we are to consider it pure joy? Because the testing of our faith produces perseverance. And when we let perseverance finish its work, we can become mature and complete, not lacking anything." (James 1:2-4)

My dad's words sank deeper into my mind with each passing second. Though I had heard that verse hundreds of times before I never really grasped the gravity of the words God was speaking. When Ryan was paralyzed had I ever stopped to consider it pure joy? Had I ever considered the testing of my faith was producing perseverance. Had I ever once thought that about what these words truly mean?

49

With those thoughts in my mind, I contemplated which really was a

better future to continue.

Chapter 7

I let my father's words sink into my soul. Maybe he was right, maybe harder didn't necessarily mean it was the worst reality. As I reflected on my life, I realized that during the most trying of times not only did I grow as a person but my faith was strengthened. In the times when I had been stripped of all that I knew, when I felt that my life couldn't get any lower, I felt closer to God than I could even put into words. When there was nothing, absolutely nothing else to hang onto other than God, he became my oxygen. When someone becomes your oxygen, you learn to rely on them for every single moment. You know that if you are not connected to them you will die. That very desperation is what has made me who I am today. If I had never known the sting of pain and loss, then I could never know how sweet it is to taste joy and peace once again.

Still surrounded by yellow tulips and my youthful father I contemplated which version of my life I wanted to continue with.

"Sunshine lets walk for a moment" and with that my dad reached for my hand and I was transported to the feeling of being a little girl, knowing the safety of my father's hand. As we walked in silence, the warmth of the sun saturated my body, and I dove into a deeper state of peace than I had ever experienced before. As we walked along, I began to see the edge of a babbling brook. The sound of water cascading over rocks filled the air.

"Let's sit," my father said as he motioned his arms towards the grass next to the brook. Quietly I did as instructed.

"You still have more time to decide which life you would like to continue. You are still in the process."
Not wanting to take my eyes off of my dad, I reluctantly closed my eyes. The sounds of the brook began to disappear as bright lights flashed in all directions. Sounds and sights whirled around me and when the spinning stopped, I was back in my house.

The shrieking cry of Maddy snapped me back into reality as I quickly jumped out of my bed and went to find her. I made my way into the nursery with pink walls in all directions. Gingham letters were hung on the wall spelling out her full name M-a-d-e-l-y-n. Her cries led me to her crib where she lay helplessly on her back crying and looking to be soothed.

"It's okay Maddy," I said as I picked her up and began rocking her back and forth. Although I was confused at which reality I was now in, I realized that she must be hungry.

I sat down on the rocking chair, lifted my shirt, and began to nurse. Stroking my sweet baby's brown hair, I wondered what this life would be like.

This must be the life where Ryan isn't hurt, I thought as I had never known a paralyzed Ryan when Maddy was born. I let out a sigh of relief as I knew in my heart that God had placed me where I belonged, safe and sound with my healthy husband. I continued rocking Maddy and thanking God for bringing me back to the reality I knew I belonged in.

My thoughts were interrupted.

"Megan, I need you" Ryan's deep voice echoed down the hallway.

What in the world, he never asks me for help I thought as I picked up Maddy and headed towards our bedroom.

My feet echoed on the hardwood floor as I made my way down the hall to our room. As I entered our bedroom my heart felt as though it was going to beat out of my chest. There where our bed usually was, I saw a large hospital type of bed. Ryan was laying down

53

looking at the ceiling as if there was no option to move his head from side to side. My eyes must be deceiving me. There was no way that what I saw in front of me could be real. No there must be some mistake! The Ryan that was there when baby Maddy was born was strong and healthy.

"What's going on," I said in a panic as I looked at the man lying in front of me. Confusion engulfed me as my eyes tried to make sense of what was happening.

"Megan, I need you to check my catheter, I think it is full."

"Wha-a-at are you talking about?" I said quickly.

"Baby, I thought you were used to this by now, you have been taking care of me for months."

Looking down at the catheter hanging off the bed I began to feel sick. I had never been good at the sight of any kind of body fluid and I felt as though I might faint.

"Ryan, how long have you been home?"

"Megs, are you sure you are feeling ok?" Ryan said while letting out a small laugh.

"Y-yes" I stammered as I reached for the catheter.

"I'll be right back," I said.

My mind was spinning from my new current reality. I hadn't a clue how to take care of my now paralyzed husband. Wanting to help my husband but not knowing how I went to Maddy's crib and laid her back down. I then found my laptop, quickly opened it and did a search for "How to change a catheter" wading through the results I quickly found a video that gave me simple step by step directions.

Heading back into our bedroom I felt more confident to complete the task ahead of me. Quickly following the directions, I had just learned I was able to empty his catheter. I stood up to survey my husband. His face was filled with whiskers from not being shaved for days. His eyes were wide open and even though his body was lifeless his eyes seemed to be filled with a supernatural life. He looked thinner than I had ever seen him, and his clothes seemed to be barely hanging on him. Where his once strong muscles used to be his shirt hung lifelessly from his body.

"To answer your question Megan, we have been home for about six months. Remember I spent a few months in rehab and then we came home before sweet Maddy was born.

"Could you bring my princess to me?" He asked.

I had been so distracted that I had almost forgotten about my baby girl. Quickly I took Maddy from her crib and held her up to Ryan. His face broke into a smile at the sight of her.

"Please, lay her on my chest" not sure what he meant I carefully laid her face down on his chest. At just two months old Maddy was still small and frail. I kept my hand on her to steady her on his chest. With every breath that Ryan took, Maddy moved up and down. She seemed calm and peaceful and I knew that she knew her daddy. She felt safe with the sound of her dad's heartbeat in her ear. She felt safe as she moved with the breathing of his lungs.

The picture before me brought tears to my eyes. My tiny helpless baby lying on my big, helpless husband. At that moment I realized what a great responsibility I had before me. They both depended on me for their every need. suddenly, I felt unbelievably inadequate.

How in the world could I take care of both of them? I can't do this! Doubt began to seep into every part of my being.

You have been created for this moment. The thought passed through my mind gently and reminded me that this was not a mistake. This moment, the moment I got married, the moment of Ryan's accident, the moment Maddy was born, I was made for this. I was purposely made for the challenge in front of me. God had equipped me with everything I would need to be successful. I would be lacking nothing as I plugged into Him. He didn't cause the accident, but He allowed it. And if He allowed it, I could accept it. I had no idea why I was brought back to the reality that included Ryan being paralyzed but I decided in that moment to embrace it. I decided to stop fighting it and let it be what it would be. I would learn to not only survive but thrive in this new reality. I would put one foot in front of the other and be the best mom and wife I could be. I knew there would be hard moments, but I was ready for it.

As if a light was shone on my situation I felt as if it was a gift that I had been chosen to be Ryan's wife and Maddy's mom. No one else on earth had my same life. No one else knew the exact pain I was in and I felt privileged that God had chosen me to be the one by Ryan's side. When I said "I do" I meant every word. I meant what I said that I would stand by my husband in sickness and in health. I meant my vows and now I was being given the chance to prove them, one day at a time.

No, this was not the life I dreamed of or the life I planned, but it was my life just the same. I knew it could have been much worse if Ryan had lost his memory or his speech. Both of those were in perfect working order which gave me hope and a new thankfulness. "This is the day that the Lord has made, I will rejoice and be glad in it" the words of a childhood Sunday school song came back into my head. I loved the perfect timing of God and how he brought things back when I needed them the most. Yes, this is the day!

Chapter 8

As the days passed, I learned to take care of not only my newborn baby but also my newly paralyzed husband. We had daily visits from nurses who would help us with the basics of life. Though Ryan had lost a lot of weight he was still too big for me to carry or help bathe. Ryan used to pride himself on never asking for help so I knew all of this must be extremely hard on him.

Each day I would let the medical team in, and they would begin performing their everyday routines. They would help Ryan out of his bed and into the bath. His favorite part of the day was when they would put him in his standing apparatus. This machine was taller than Ryan and helped put him into a standing position. That day there was a particular glimmer in Ryan's eyes as he joked with everyone around him. "Today I almost feel like a normal person" he laughed as his body was placed into a standing position.

As he was placed into the machine which was a sort of treadmill that would make his feet slowly and mechanically form steps in what had become his own version of walking.

"At this rate I'll be doing a marathon soon" Ryan said with a smile. The nurse and I laughed, I loved seeing Ryan in a good mood. He lived for these moments when he could stand and almost feel normal again.

Watching my husband do his own version of walking, I thought about how blessed we were that he had not lost his memory. *What if he hadn't remembered me? What if he was not able to talk or communicate in any way?* Things could have been a lot worse.

Observing my husband walk I got lost deep in thought. I realized that all we had been through was so much bigger than just ourselves. Our lives had affected so many people that I knew and so many more that I didn't know.

I had always enjoyed keeping in touch with friends and family via social media. One day a few months before Ryan's accident I was on a run. I had turned off my music and heard a still small voice. Though the voice was not audible, but I heard it very clearly. *You are going to go through something difficult and I want you to do it publicly.* *What,* I thought? What in the world is going to happen? It was such a clear instruction that it almost scared me.

So, there I was going through the hardest time of my life and I was using social media as a way to share it with the world. I tried to be raw and open yet still protect my husband. He tended to be a more private person so sharing his updates was at first difficult for him. He learned to see the sharing of his life as a way for more people to pray for him and a way for more lives to be touched with how we were handling all of this.

One day I was feeling particularly sad, but I felt like God wanted me to share the real, raw, truth. I was never big about going out in public with my glasses on, but I knew I had to share as I was, glasses or not. With my makeup-less face, I turned on my live feed to social media. As the number watching began to increase so did the pace of my heart. I titled my video "Real and Raw" and with the push of a button I was live and open to the views of the world. Trying not to look at myself as I recorded, I sniffled and began. Tears flowing down my face I tried to make words form. "Hey friends, I wanted to thank you for taking this journey with us. You have faithfully prayed and been there for us through these past months, it's getting closer to a year now and I want you to know we appreciate each one of you. I know I am not looking my best right now" I said as I looked down uncomfortably.

"But I wanted to share with you now, while the feelings and emotions are still raw and real. You guys, I am not going to lie, seeing my husband like this is the hardest thing I have ever had to do.

Watching him learn to move again and never be able to do the things he once loved like running and swimming and hiking nearly breaks my heart daily." The tears began to flow even more freely now. "Yes, this is the hardest thing I have ever had to endure but I know that I know that I know that God has prepared me for this. Me, the person who used to faint at the sight of the smallest amount of blood, me that used to run from hospitals, me that once got sick at the thought of anything painful.

Yes, that same person has now been chosen to walk by Ryan's side. I don't know why God chose me, but he did. Sometimes I am reminded that God uses the most unlikely people for his most important jobs. Moses who stuttered led the Israelites towards the promised land, God even used a donkey to speak. Friends, I used to cry out to God over and over simply saying "Why" I repeated this over and over. Honestly, there was a time when I struggled with anger. I was so mad at God. As I fell deeper into my pit of anger a good friend looked me in the eyes and said "Megan, you are too good for this, what are you doing?" that friend woke me up out of my pit of self-pity. I stopped saying why and I started saying "God, I do not understand this pain we are in. I do not understand why you allowed my husband who is just 26 years old to become paralyzed. But, God, if you allowed it then I can accept it. It doesn't mean that I like it, but I accept it. I accept that you chose me. Me! Of all people, you chose me to be Ryan's wife and walk by him in all this pain.

In all this earth-shattering reality, you chose me. You guys, I want to encourage you, whatever situation you are in, God is with you. The other day he brought a verse to my mind and I have such a strong image in my mind of it. The waters are all around, yet He parted them, and I am able to walk through. He makes ways when there seems to be no other way. The verse I read was 2 Samuel 22:17 " He reached down from on high and took hold of me: he drew me out of deep waters" and I can tell you I am living proof that He can restore and save someone from utter darkness.

When I was a little girl, just ten years old I lost my father to cancer. When he died, I felt a part of me died right alongside of him. When I said goodbye to him, when I watched him struggle to take his last breath, I felt like I might die right alongside of him. At ten years old I hadn't ever known such heartache, such depths of sadness that grief can bring, I had never yet understood the weight of grief. I got through it and I know it made me a stronger person, I know it has made me the person you see today. I know without that experience I might not know how to survive the weight of what is happening with my dear sweet Ryan.

That horrific experience prepared me to stand by my husband's side. I watched my mom do it. She was an example of how to love in sickness and in health and her example is what has helped me today to stand by my man. Hey mom, if you're watching, thank you" I said as I wiped a single tear from my face. "Thank you for supporting us, I have some specific prayer requests. As you obviously know Ryan can no longer work and I can't work right now with a newborn and my responsibilities of taking care of Ryan. Please pray that we will make it financially, we have a mortgage payment and other bills staring us in the face that we have no idea how in the world we are going to pay. I am not worried, God always provides for our every need even if we must wait until the last minute to receive it, He has never failed us yet. Also please pray for the peace of mind as Ryan goes through this excruciating process both physically and mentally of being permanently paralyzed. It is an uphill battle every day. Well, I think that is all I have for you today, we love you."

I hit the end button and let go of the results of what would become of the video. I did what I knew I was supposed to and shared with the world. Now it was up to God with what He wanted to do with it.

Maddy's cry interrupted my thoughts as I walked towards her nursery to get her. Her cry comforted me that I was not alone. What if Ryan's accident had happened before I was pregnant? There would be no Maddy. Though Maddy demanded what little energy I had left after caring for Ryan, she was my everything. My world and life would not be complete without her. Maddy could melt my heart in a nanosecond. One look at her face and I melted into a puddle. What a gift and blessing she was.

When life was hard, it was hard to see or feel any joy. In the hardest of moments, I had a difficult time considering things pure joy. When my mind and body felt like I had been through a blender it was hard to really consider it pure joy. The closer I grew to God the quicker and easier it became for me to react with joy.

Chapter 9

As the days went on I tried to shake the feeling that I was in a dream. The feeling of floating through the minutes and hours seemed to never leave. With the sunrise each day came the feelings of love for my Maddy and Ryan, but also a strong sense that this couldn't be my life. After posting the video of me crying and sharing my raw emotions I received countless texts and phone calls. Over and over were the same words, "You and Ryan are so strong, you are such an inspiration, I don't know how you do it." The strange thing about receiving those messages was that so many times I would still feel so alone. Even those closest to me seemed to be distant because they did not understand what it was like to be living with my new reality. Even the most well-meaning people made me feel alone. In the beginning I cried myself to sleep and cried all day.

As the months continued and I settled into my new role as mother and caretaker there were days when I almost felt numb. There were days when I had nothing to look forward to but diaper changes and catheter cleanings.

I was completely and utterly sucked dry of joy. I looked in the mirror and no longer recognized myself. I used to be so full of joy and fun, often known as the life of the party.

Staring in the mirror I said "Megan, what are you doing? You still have two people who love you so much and need you today, this day" more words came into my head " You are my hiding place; you will protect me from trouble and surround me with songs of deliverance."

(Psalm 32:7 | NIV)

Megan- oh Megan you have not been seeking the Lord, you have not been using him as your hiding place. It is time to start seeking God and His strength instead of your own. I realized at that moment that I had been trying to be everything to everyone in my own strength. I had not been hiding in God's love and peace and I certainly hadn't been finding joy each day. "It is time I change how I am living and start having joy no matter what my circumstances were. I learned as a child in Sunday School the difference between joy and happiness. Happiness is based on circumstances while joy is based on God. It was the only explanation of how you could witness people in even the hardest of conditions have joy and smiles on their faces. I realized that along with Ryan being paralyzed I had been having paralyzed joy.

I no longer let my joy shine through but had been living stuck in my circumstances. I resolved to change my heart and stay letting the joy of God live full in my life. I knew it didn't mean that life would be easy, but I knew life would be better relying on God.

"The joy of the Lord is my strength," I said aloud as I looked in the mirror and for the first time in a long time I smiled at myself, not a fake trying to mask the pain smile but a genuine joy of the Lord smile.

"Megan" Ryan's voice broke my thoughts as I quickly walked towards our bedroom.

"Yes, baby, what is it?"

"Can you help me sit up and bring Maddy in here? I want to see her play"

"Sure, let me help," I said as I pushed the button on the side of his bed and heard the sound of his bed lifting him up.

"Let me go get Maddy."

As I approached Maddy's crib she was sitting up and a huge smile came on her face. She reached for me and said "Mama"

No matter how many times I heard her sweet voice utter those words it melted my heart. I kissed her on her rosy cheek and carried her to our bedroom. I brought her head to Ryan's lips and he kissed her gently.

68

"Dada" she nearly sang. Madelyn Joy, we had surely named her the right thing as she brought joy to our lives in a time when we needed it the most.

We set up a playpen for Maddy that was in Ryan's sightline when he was in a sitting position. This had easily become the highlight of his day. Reaching for a, plush butterfly, Maddy squealed in delight. I had heard from other moms about how fussy or hard their babies were, but not our Maddy. I was so thankful to have such a happy and content baby.

"Maddy, Daddy loves you so very much, who loves you?
"Daddy does," Ryan said in his best baby talk.

As the sun cascaded in through the windows for the first time in what seemed like forever, I felt the feeling of joy. No, these were not the circumstances I would ever have chosen for myself, Ryan, or Maddy but I had learned to be content and to find joy even in the hardest of times. Yes, my dreams for the future of more babies and traveling were over and I started thinking I was on plan B. But what if my plan B was really God's plan A? What if he knew all along that this would be my life? What if this was the way it was always supposed to be? What if God in all his sovereignty had let me experience this so I could know the pure joy of the testing of my faith, that it would bring perseverance and make me complete into who he created me to be?

With a mind shift, I began to contemplate the talk I had, had with my dad in heaven. His words began to make sense in my head as I realized that without the current wrestling and troubles, I would not be who I was supposed to be and neither would Maddy or Ryan. Deep in thought, I contemplated what really grasping this concept would mean. It would mean that I could let go of the negativity and wake up realizing that this is joy. It is a joy to face troubles and hardships and worries and pain. What if the whole world could understand this concept? Why do we avoid pain and trials like they are the worst thing to ever happen to us? If we honestly believed God's word, believed it with every fiber in our being, we would welcome trouble. We would welcome the pain because we know it is ultimately for His glory and to make us into better people along the way.

Tears slipped down my face as I realized all the times I had fought the pain. All the times I had tried to run from it, hide from it and never face it head-on. I couldn't change the past, but I could change the future. I let the words find their way deep into my soul "Consider it pure joy when you face trials." Pure joy, like the joy I feel when I see Maddy smile or call me Mama, pure joy like the feeling of my family safe in one room, pure joy, like God has when he looks at me. Joy does not come from myself; it is only God's supernatural power that can infuse me daily with joy when the world looks the bleakest. Only his Strength can power me through the day and help me to overcome even the darkest times.

I reflected on the morning I woke up with the realization that my husband was paralyzed and my life was forever changed, that I had my perspective wrong, that I didn't get it, I didn't get that the trials were a gift. My mind was reeling from this new discovery, this new way of thinking, this new way of living. I wanted to shout it from the rooftops to people, I didn't want people to feel sorry for me anymore because I was given such a beautiful, divine gift, God wanted me to be complete and lacking nothing.

Why had God allowed me to see both versions of my life? I used to believe the other version where Ryan had not had the accident was for sure the one I should continue. But now I had, had a paradigm shift, a discovery, an awakening, How could I go back to a life with so much less pain and hardships if I knew that it wouldn't develop perseverance and character in me.

How could I go back knowing all the gifts because of the pain? This was becoming more complicated with every passing day. In the beginning, the decision was easy. I wanted to avoid pain at all costs, but I had come to realize that in the pain we become the best version of ourselves if we let go of everything else and cling to God so very tightly. When I am emptied and void of relying on others and myself, when I am stripped down to nothing but my soul and my need for God it is only then that I can be completely filled with his peace and rely on him for every step and every breath. This need would never be here if all my problems were gone.

With this new resolve, I thanked God for giving me the pain of today and the pain of tomorrow and I prayed that Ryan would come to his own realization of this and someday Maddy would grasp this concept as well. With Ryan and myself as examples, I prayed that she would understand this at a young age and live up to her middle name of Joy. Madelyn Joy Montgomery, our little angel.

Chapter 10

The moment that I truly embraced considering trials pure joy I got hit with another blow. I literally felt like I had been hit by a semi-truck. I could hear the cries of my sweet husband from the living room. I quickly ran to our bedroom and came to his side on the bed.

"What is it?" I asked as I touched his face knowing it was the only place, he could physically feel my touch.

"I just want to die, why didn't God just let me die?" Ryan yelled with his eyes closed tight. The pain seemed to seep from his pores as he continued.

"I hate this, I hate this. I want to move but I can't. I want to embrace you; I want to pick up Maddy. I want to walk; I want to be human again!" Tears were now freely flowing as his chest heaved in and out. His breathing became faster and faster as he struggled to find his breath. I could see he was having the beginning of a panic attack.

"It's okay baby, it's okay, take a deep breath. Breathe with me now."

I began breathing slowly, trying to get him to match the rhythm of my breath. I continued breathing in and out while gently touching his face so he could feel the comfort of physical touch.

His breathing began to slow, and I felt as though my heart might break. The words "Consider it pure joy came into my mind. *Are you kidding me, God? How in the world do I consider it pure joy when THIS is the situation my husband is in when this is the life we now must accept? How can my husband's tears be considered pure joy?* It was such a confusing concept because while I knew I was to consider it pure joy I also knew that God weeps when we weep, so he feels our pain. He loved Ryan even more than I did which was hard to imagine.

"Ryan, I am so sorry you are going through all this. I can't even imagine what it is like feeling trapped inside a body that won't do what you want it to do. I can't relate to you about that, but I can relate that I know what it is like to have my life totally altered in a second. I know what it's like to be totally and completely devastated. I am so very sorry Ryan."

The man who tried so awfully hard to keep his emotions tucked behind his tough exterior continued crying and let out his thoughts and pain.

"Oh, Megs what is the point of life now? What am I supposed to do? I can't be a lawyer from here! I can't do what I went to school for? How could this be God's plan? How could he let this happen?" Listening intently and carefully considering my word choice I prayed about how to respond to my pain-stricken husband.

Remember Megan, I chose you for this journey. I chose you for this role, I will give you the words to speak. God's words reminded me that I was never alone, never alone in my thoughts or prayers or words.

"Ryan, I don't know yet what the plan is for your life, for our life, for Maddy's life but I know that we have today. Today you are alive and well. God must have some kind of plan and purpose for your life."

Ryan's breathing had begun to slow, and his crying had subsided.

"What do you think I am supposed to do now?"

"Ryan, I am not sure but we will pray for an answer to that question and seek and seek God. For now, your job is to be the best dad and husband you can be and you are already doing a good job at that" I said with a smile.

"I think I would like to watch a sermon now, could you help me?" My brother had recently installed a tv on our ceiling. It had been so great for Ryan to be able to keep up with his favorite sports teams, news, favorite shows, and sermons.

I knew exactly which sermon would be good for us to see once again. We both loved this pastors' sermons as they were totally relatable to what we were going through. This one was titled "If God allowed it, I can accept it" We often quoted the title to each other when we had a hard time accepting our current reality. The pastor enthusiastically made his way from one end of the stage to another often jumping around with a passion for the words he was preaching. His kind of passion was contagious. He had a take on life that I appreciated. He wasn't all proper with his speaking style, he was just an ordinary man with an extraordinary calling.

I studied Ryan's face as he watched the screen. Just like Ryan, I thought. An ordinary man with an extraordinary calling. He was going down one path at his Law firm and now he would have the opportunity to find his new calling. He would have the chance to explore new ways for God to use him. I don't believe that God allowed all this pain and hardship to happen just to have Ryan alone in his room and alone in his pain for the rest of his life. No, there was something more here and I was going to help Ryan find it. It may not be big or glamourous and definitely didn't include jumping around a stage but just as big in purpose.

My mind was spinning with ideas. Maybe Ryan could dictate words to me and he could write a book, or maybe he could learn to paint with his mouth or even learn to use a computer with his mouth with a device I had seen on YouTube. I had spent many hours learning about other people's stories of being paralyzed and what things in technology had helped them and what amazing inventions had been created in aiding them to have the most normal life possible.

As Ryan continued watching the sermon, I was lost in thoughts of the future. Where the future used to look like a deep black hole, I suddenly saw light cracking its way through the darkness as hope began to rise. Ideas for the future made it easier to face. I felt excitement an emotion I could barely remember feeling creeping back up inside of me. This was not the end; this was just the beginning.

Ryan's future had a lot of possibilities and options. I would patiently help him discover them in his own time. I knew if I pushed the issue it would not work. I had to love him through the process and be by his side as he went through it.

With the sermon flowing I closed my eyes and began to feel myself relax a little. I closed my eyes, bright lights flashed and images swirled and the now familiar feeling of traveling through space and time came over me once again as I knew what was happening. I opened my eyes and was once again surrounded by yellow tulips for as far as my eyes could see. The vibrancy of the color of the yellow was something richer and more intense than anything I had ever seen on earth before. I inhaled deeply and all the worries and fears were once again completely gone.

I stood up and wondered who or what would greet me this time. This time was different, I didn't see anyone or hear anyone's voice. I began walking straight ahead. I had a feeling that I can't explain, it was like peace but deeper and stronger than anything I had ever experienced. Step after step and time felt like it was standing still. I had no idea how much time went by as I walked in peaceful bliss. In the distance, I could see some kind of animal by a stream.

As I got closer, I saw that it was a deer. I could tell it was a fawn and it was brown with small white spots. I thought of a verse I learned long ago " As the deer pants for streams of water, so my soul pants for you, my God" Psalm 42:1 Seeing the deer and experiencing the peace I saw the verse in a new light. As much as the deer needed the flowing water of the stream so my soul needed to be with God. As I got closer to the deer drinking from the stream I heard once again the deep and soothing voice surrounding me in all directions.

"Megan, I see you seeking me just as this deer seeks the water." I see how much you are relying on me for your every need. You are doing a good job. I see you growing and prospering, I see you considering the trials pure joy and I am very pleased. You are becoming the person I created you to be." Unable to speak I continued listening.

"I have been letting you experience two kinds of lives for a purpose. You have been doing so well. I still want you to go back and experience a little more before making your final decision." and with the last syllable of his word, the world began to spin again.

I suddenly woke to the sound of a screeching alarm clock. The bright red letters read six AM as I looked around confused. Suddenly I felt the covers move and I saw Ryan quickly get out of bed and stand up. The site of my husband standing took me by surprise and I couldn't hold back my tears. What was happening, was I still dreaming?

"Good morning Megs," He said as he leaned down to kiss me. And with that I realized I was back in the reality that included a happy and healthy Ryan.

Chapter 11

S till in shock at the sight of Ryan standing up and walking, I stared in disbelief. My emotions were all over the place going back and forth between my lives. I could hear the sounds of Ryan in the kitchen, suddenly I heard sweet Maddy's cry. I went to her nursery surprised to see an older Maddy, she appeared to be about 1 year old.

"Mama, Mama, Mama" I heard her little voice say as I approached her crib. The older she got the more she resembled Ryan. I looked into her deep brown mini-me Ryan eyes and smiled. Picking her up, I walked into the kitchen. Ryan was eating a bowl of cereal and reading the newspaper.

"Hey Megs, don't wait for me for dinner tonight, you know I have that huge case I am working on and will be at work late tonight," Ryan said without even looking up from the paper.

"Okay" I replied hesitantly, not fully knowing what he was talking about. I set Maddy in her highchair and poured some cheerios for her. As her chubby little fingers reached for the cheerios, I watched as she tried to pick one up and then another. Mind reeling, I surveyed my current reality.

I observed that all the things in the kitchen looked like they had before. The only things that I could see that had changed were Ryan and Maddy. Within just a few minutes Ryan put his bowl in the sink and kissed me and Maddy.

He quickly said goodbye and with that, he was out the door.

It felt so good to see Ryan walking. The alternate realities were both amazing and painful.

"I guess it's just you and me baby girl," I said smiling at Maddy. She smiled back at me and I was so thankful to have her in my life. While Ryan had changed in my different realities my sweet baby Maddy was my constant. Just a glimpse of her face could cheer me up. She was a ray of sunshine amidst my pain and confusion.

"Thank you, God," I whispered aloud.

I spent the day playing with Maddy, doing laundry, and cleaning the house. The mindless tasks of scrubbing toilets and washing windows kept me occupied throughout the day. The day stretched into evening and I began to feel lonely. At least in my other life, Ryan was always with me. Here he was healthy, but he was not with his family. Praying that today was a rare exception I continued working around the house.

The evening continued and I laid Maddy down to sleep. Singing along with the lullaby that was playing in her room a tear fell down my face. *This was so strange, I thought that if I had a healthy husband, I would be happy, why did I feel so lost, so alone?*

The clock read 8:00 pm and Ryan still was not home. I picked up my phone and called him. After four rings it went to voicemail. I hung up quickly. *This is crazy* I thought, *why does he work so much*? I went to the bedroom and turned on the tv, trying to distract myself with reality tv where I could get lost in other people's worlds. I must have dozed off because I woke up to the sound of the garage door opening and the familiar hum of Ryan's truck entering the garage. Ryan walked into the room, loosening his tie, and taking off his shoes.
"How was work?" I asked

"Oh, ya know, another day, another dollar," Ryan replied with a clearly annoyed tone. I knew that talking to him at this point would not do any good. What happened to the happy Ryan I married? Even the paralyzed Ryan was happier than this shadow of the Ryan that I married that I saw before me. I closed my eyes and returned to sleeping.

I woke to the sound of the screeching alarm clock once again. Once again the clock read 6:00 am. I watched through half-closed eyes as Ryan got dressed and started getting ready for work. The day seemed to start the same as the previous day.He went to the kitchen and I sat up and surveyed the current situation. Yes, I loved that he was healthy and well but he seemed to be a workaholic. He didn't smile as much as paralyzed Ryan even though he was much healthier. I was having a hard time wrapping my head around this new reality. If paralyzed Ryan could see healthy Ryan he would want to shake him and say " Wake up, you have it so good! You can walk and run and pick up your baby girl yet you barely even smile." That is what I felt like saying.

The days continued in almost the same fashion every single day. Ryan woke up, had breakfast headed to work and came home about 8 or 9 pm. He would shower, watch a few shows, fall asleep and do it all over again. Weekends didn't even vary very much from weekdays. He slept in a little later, ate breakfast and later headed to the office to work extra on his most urgent cases.

I thought that Sundays would be different as the Ryan that I knew and loved was always eager to attend church. On the first Sunday with healthy Ryan when he woke up, I asked him which service he wanted to attend. He looked at me like I was an alien.

"Meg's you know I don't go to church anymore. I can't believe you would even ask me that, are you feeling okay?" He looked at me with his eyes squinting. My mind was reeling trying to figure out why in the world he would not want to go to church. I decided to let it go for the time being.

I went and got Maddy from her crib and dressed her in her cutest frilly pink dress. She repeated "Mama, Mama" over and over again and reached for my face. Her adorable smile and dimples were enough to melt me every time.

"Let's go to church," I said.

"Go church" she repeated in her sweet little voice. I laughed aloud as I picked her up and carried her into the kitchen. After eating breakfast I called out,

"Bye Ryan, we will see you later" I closed the front door behind me and headed to the car. Buckling Maddy into her car seat I got ready to drive to church. *This sure was a strange reality.* I thought. *So very strange, is this really the life I wanted? A healthy husband, but at what cost? This Ryan worked all the time and he barely noticed me and Maddy. How could he ignore the sweetest girl on earth? How could he not want to spend every second with her?*

Pulling into the church parking lot I was happy that I had a church I loved, even if I had to go without Ryan. I walked into the familiar building, took Maddy to the nursery and found my seat in the back of the sanctuary. Worship songs always had a way of penetrating my soul. The combination of the music, the words and the undeniable presence of God, I was almost always moved to tears. It was an experience that was difficult to put into words. The closest I could come to explain to others about what the presence of the Holy Spirit was like the feeling of floating. Like a warm blanket placed over me and then I was rising in the air, higher and higher as I closed my eyes in worship. This was always the highlight of my week, with or without Ryan, I always enjoyed spending time in worship and at church. After several songs, the music ended and the pastor came to the podium.

As he began to speak, I felt like God was speaking directly to me, it was crazy how many times I felt like the message was tailor-made for me. He spoke of the promises of God, how God would never leave me nor forsake me. He would always be near me and close to me. He would never leave me or ignore me the way Ryan had. He would be by my side no matter what. There were times that Ryan made me feel invisible. He barely looked at me anymore and I don't remember the last time that I saw him smile. His dimples were barely visible anymore and he never seemed interested in anything other than work.

God I need your help, I desperately need your help. This person was not who I married. Sure he wasn't physically paralyzed but he seemed emotionally paralyzed. Like someone who has such a gift in front of him but didn't even realize it. Suddenly it came to me- this Ryan had never had the trials of health to consider it pure joy. Because he had not known the same trials, he had not been tested to the point of perseverance, he didn't have the perseverance to finish its work in him and make his faith complete.

I almost felt sorry for.him. He had not been through the fire, He was not molded into the person I saw paralyzed Ryan become. He had not had the pure joy of constant trials. Work was the only thing he had to sometimes give him trials, he didn't have the trial of health or finances or really anything big, he had a good job, wonderful wife and amazing baby girl. But in all these gifts he had not been tested. So without the testing, his faith had not become complete and lacking nothing. With this new realization, I hoped to have the opportunity to show him the gifts that he had right in front of his face.

Chapter 12

I returned home from church to find Ryan watching a football game on TV.

"Hi," I said as I handed Maddy to him and began the mindless activity of cooking lunch, his favorite grilled cheese, and tomato soup. Suddenly I looked at Ryan and said

"Ryan, are you happy?" He looked away from the tv stunned.

"Of course, I am happy," he replied. He returned his eyes instantly to the tv screen.

"No, I mean really happy?"

"Sure, why are you bringing this up?" he said with an annoyed sound in his voice.

'You just work a lot and I hardly see you smile. When you come home you are too exhausted to spend time with Maddy and I. I just want to see you happy"

'Why are you nagging me, woman!" Ryan glared at me. I was shocked by his demeaning words and tone.

"I am sorry, I am not trying to nag you, I just wonder if you realize how awful life would be if you were, say paralyzed or had some other kind of sickness."

Ryan stared at me as though I was completely insane.

"Well that will never happen," he said as he shut off the TV with the remote and stormed out of the room.

A few minutes later he appeared in the living room again.

"I'm going to the gym," he said as he slammed the door behind him and headed to his truck. As the engine started and I watched him drive away I felt a new kind of sadness. Why was he so angry? What had happened to him, or more like what was happening or had not happened to him?

Maddy woke up from her afternoon nap and I decided to take her for a walk. The fall air was getting cooler, but I knew the fresh air would do us both good. Bundling Maddy up in her warmest coat and piling blankets on her in the stroller we set off on our walk. I loved the way the leaves were beginning to change colors and drop to the ground. Vivid orange and yellow leaves surrounded us as we made our way to our neighborhood trail.

The crisp air felt good on my face as I began to walk. How could this life be so much less happy? This was backward of what I thought was ever possible. I guess he didn't realize how good he had it because he had never had his health taken away. As I walked down the path, I began to see a strange sight. Was I dreaming? Where the trees ended a field of bright yellow tulips began. They looked so out of place in the fall wonderland we had been walking through.

"What in the world?" I said aloud as I walked closer to the field of tulips. The tulips reminded me of the times I had been to heaven. Stepping into the field, I closed my eyes and bright lights surrounded me in all directions. The world started to spin, and I knew what was happening. This sensation had happened so often that I now knew what it was.

I let the process complete. I felt the warmth and peace of the sun and knew I was once again in heaven. Opening my eyes, I was still in a field of tulips, but this one so much brighter than the one on earth. The unmistakable peace that enveloped me only when I was in this place covered my entire body. As I opened my eyes, I could see people surrounding me in all directions. I spun around and realized that I was surrounded in the middle of a circle of people. The people were too far away to see their faces, but I could see they were holding up signs.

Sounds were coming from them; the noises began to get clearer and I realized they were cheering. Some were jumping up and down and some were pumping their arms in victory. I observed that every single one of them was completely engaged in cheering for something or someone. Totally overwhelmed and very confused I walked out of the center of the circle and towards one of the sides of people surrounding me. With each step, their cheering got louder. "You can do it" I heard very clearly.

"We love you and believe in you!" another voice said.

"Goooooo Megan" I heard another voice say in almost a song-like tone.

Wait, what, I thought, suddenly I realized they were cheering for me. *Wow, this is pretty amazing* I thought. *But why? Why are all these people cheering for me?* stepping closer to the voices I heard the distinct sound of a voice I would recognize anywhere, the sound of my grandpa Ben. My grandpa Ben had died when I was twelve. He was my father's dad and watching his son suffer with cancer and eventually pass away seemed to take the life right out of him. His heart broke right along with mine and he never seemed to recover. Though he was sad he was a great man of God. He was always there with a verse and a word of encouragement. He had a deep, loud voice that you could always hear from everywhere in his house.

As I walked closer, I studied his face. Just like my father's face was younger in heaven so was my grandpa Ben's. He had the same olive complexion of my father as well as similar deep brown eyes and dimples to match his smile.

"Grandpa Ben?" I said as I wrapped my arms around his neck and hugged him.

"Yes, it's me sweet girl" his low voice bellowed.

"What, what are you doing?" I said surveying the circle of those surrounding me and cheering.

"Oh Megan, we love you so much! We are cheering you on!" He said with an enthusiastic look on his face.

"Why in the world are you cheering? You guys are acting like this is the Olympics!" I said still trying to make sense of what was happening.

Suddenly I was distracted by the beautiful woman by his side. The stunning jawbone and piercing blue eyes stopped me in my tracks. My heart pounded faster at the realization of who was in front of me.

"Grandma Vera?" I wrapped my arms around the youthful neck of my favorite grandma with tears streaming down my face. I had always been told I looked like my grandma Vera and seeing before me a young woman I could see it even stronger than I ever had before. My eyes were a different color but our other features were almost identical. I had always wished I knew my grandma better. I was just three years old when she passed away from heart failure.

Even though I was only three when she died, I had some very strong memories of her and I always loved the fact that people said I looked like her. I mourned the loss of her as I was growing up that I had never had the chance to get to know her. But here she was directly in front of me. Shocked I stepped back to look at her again. Her hair was elegantly pulled back in a side braid and wrapped into a bun. She looked just like the picture I had seen of her when she was just seventeen years old. I had always felt a deep connection to this woman I had barely known.

She looked at me intently "Megan, I have always loved you and watched over you. You are such a treasure and I have had the privilege of seeing all of your special moments. I have loved watching you grow and also grow in your faith. I have never stopped being on team Megan and I have been cheering you on every day of your life." Intently studying her face, she continued

"You haven't always had it easy and I know that sometimes you have felt alone in your pain, but God is always with you. Always. And you have all of us" she said as she motioned around the circle. "You have all of us who cheer you on and believe in you" I glanced around the circle and began to recognize more faces of people that had already gone to heaven. Not wanting to leave her but wanting to see who else was there I looked to her left.

"Chris!" I exclaimed in shock. The face of a close friend from college eagerly greeted me. Chris looked just like he did the last time I saw him. He had not aged at all, as he was sadly one of my friends who had died way too young. His still twenty-two-year-old face shone brightly as his smile lit up just like it always had. His eyes seemed to twinkle as I stared at him in disbelief.

"Hey Megan, good to see you!" Chris said as we hugged. Chris had died unexpectedly shortly after we graduated from college. I had never understood why God had allowed such an amazing, vibrant, and full of life young man to leave earth so soon. His death was the first time I had experienced someone my own age dying. It was the first time I really came to realize that I would never understand and the first time I started believing that if God allowed it I could accept it. Chris was always such a good friend to me. I started college in the spring and he quickly befriended me and made me feel welcome. He never ceased to amaze me with his zest for life and love for adventures.

"So good to see you too. Why are you cheering for me?" I asked, genuinely trying to understand why I was surrounded by friends and family who were yelling my name or holding up signs with my name on it.

"Megan, we are privileged to be part of your cheering team, your great cloud of witnesses"
A verse I had heard hundreds of times but never really comprehended came into my mind. It was about being surrounded by a great cloud of witnesses and how they were cheering me on.

I suddenly realized that the people surrounding me were encouraging me on in my life. They were cheering to help me persevere. They were part of God's gift to me of people already in heaven who were on my team. Special people to give me hope in the hardest times. I had heard this verse interpreted in different ways but this way made the most sense to me and was another example of how much God loves us. The sound of a guitar filled the air and I witnessed Chris passionately strumming a guitar the way I had seen him do hundreds of times before. He closed his eyes and began to sing. Soon all the others   joined him. It was the most beautiful display of worship I had ever seen or heard.

"I love you Lord and I lift my voice to worship you, oh my soul rejoice" the Angelic chorus continued.

"Take joy my king in what you hear may it be a sweet, sweet sound in your ear"

There were no words to describe the level of peace I was feeling. The sound of the people I loved in sweet harmony praising God was enough to bring me to my knees. I joined my great cloud of witnesses in worship and felt a stronger connection to God than I had ever experienced before.

Chapter 13

As the song ended, I opened my eyes to see the people in the circle around me. As I turned around, I saw my youthful father again. I ran across the circle and yelled "Daddy" as I wrapped my arms around him.

"Hey, Sunshine it is good to see you again!"

"You too Daddy" I stood back surveying his youthful face again. The worry lines on his face were now gone and I loved seeing him pain-free. When he was on the earth and towards the end of his days, I remember feeling so helpless as he would cry out in pain. Each time I would hear his cry I would run to my room put my face down in the pillow and scream as loud as I could.

Though I was screaming with all my might, just a faint muffled sound could be heard.

"God, please make the pain stop" I would yell aloud.

Over and over this would happen and each time my cries were met with silence. One day a friend told me that God sees all of our pain and that he actually saves our tears in a bottle. Thinking my friend must have her facts wrong, I turned in my pink faux leather Bible to the back to find the concordance. These were the days; long before the internet and this is how we looked things up. I found the word tears and it told me to turn to Psalm 56:8 *"You keep track of all my sorrows. You have collected all my tears in your bottle. You have recorded each one in your book."* (NLT)

That verse made a lasting impact as I actually began to visualize God wiping the tears off of my face and placing them in a large bottle. I used to picture how full my bottle must be. What a loving God to care enough to collect our tears. Studying my youthful daddy again I realized how thankful I was to see him again.

"Okay Sunshine, you have had a little more time, how is it going with healthy Ryan?"

"Daddy, I think you might have been right, maybe the pain does make us into who we are supposed to be. Maybe the accident really helped him to be a better person. The Ryan I am living with is so unhappy! Daddy I thought since he isn't paralyzed, he would be happy. All he does is work and then when comes home late from work he is so grumpy; he doesn't even go to church anymore. Even though he isn't paralyzed he doesn't seem to realize how good he has it. He has me and Maddy, but it is like we are invisible. It's so backward of what I thought it would be like. "

"Yes, Sunshine, sometimes our pain does make us into who we are supposed to be. Let's talk about you for a minute" He said looking intently into my eyes.

"You went through one of the hardest things anyone ever has to go through, and you did it as a child. You lost your father, me at just ten years old. I know it broke your heart, but did it make you become stronger?"

Thinking about my words carefully I began

"Yes, I believe it did. I went through a period of unthinkable pain, but in that pain, I began to know my heavenly father in a deeper way than I ever had before. The pain of losing you left a hole in my heart. But God came and filled that hole. It was never the same without you but I learned a new normal and I learned how to have joy even while in pain."

"So you would say it helped shape you into the woman I see before me?"

"Yes, I would never have chosen to lose you, but I do see it as an example of God making beauty out of ashes, he was able to redeem me in ways that would never have been possible if you had been there. So I can see that Ryan has no idea how bad his life could be and therefore he is taking his health for granted. I used to think that I should continue the way it is now, but I am not so sure. It would be perfect if I could get him to see how amazing he has it. Maybe, that's it, maybe I need to go back and try to get him to see that he is a blessed man!" I said with a new excitement.

Maybe I could have the best of both worlds, maybe I could have a healthy and happy husband. That was what I dreamed of when I got married, that is what I thought I was signing up for.

"In my experience, you cannot change someone my Sunshine." God is the only one who can change someone and even then, he never forces them but guides them and lets them choose for themselves. He gives us the gift of free will. So just be careful thinking you can change him" With that, he put his arm around me as we walked through the field of yellow tulips.

Suddenly I realized all the people had disappeared and I was alone with my dad.

"I know Daddy, but I have to at least try. If I want to be married to a happy and healthy husband, I have to try to help him be happy. So this is the best chance of making it work."

"Alright," My father replied hesitantly. I could tell he didn't think it was the best idea, but he always seemed to let me make my own choices and decisions on earth and now in heaven.

"Actually, I wish I could stay here with you," I said looking into my dad's deep brown eyes.

"I know, and someday you will be here with me, but your time on earth is not done yet. God still has plans for your life, and I know you will make the most out of every day and complete what God has for you"

He kissed the top of my head and my world began to swirl again and I knew it was time for me to return home. I was getting used to visiting heaven and I found that every time I left, I missed it a little more. There was a serene peace that couldn't be found anywhere else.

There were no words to explain how I felt when I was there. I had read about heaven and almost became obsessed about learning about heaven when my father died, but none of the books or stories I ever heard came even close to describing what heaven was actually like. It was impossible to explain in earthly words a heavenly realm. As the lights flashed and my world spun, I wondered where I would end up. I closed my eyes and let the process continue. I opened my eyes and found myself in my bed, I looked to my left and saw Ryan sleeping soundly next to me.

Okay, I had the chance again to help him realize that he has things pretty good. I stared at the ceiling and contemplated how I could get my point across.

100

The screeching sound of the alarm clock interrupted my thoughts. The clock read 6:00 am as Ryan got up and started his usual morning routine. I watched him rise, put on his suit and tie and head to the kitchen. My mind was reeling with ways to help healthy Ryan appreciate his life.

I could show him some videos about those who were paralyzed, I thought as I recalled some recent videos I saw. No, that wouldn't work, he needed to feel it a little more. I could try to find someone in the hospital he could visit. Hmm, I could start working on that one. Or, maybe I should just tell him that I had seen what he was like paralyzed. No way, he would think I was totally nuts, I mean who would believe that not only had I experienced two versions of my life but I had also visited heaven several times. Yep, no way that would work.

Distracted by the sound of Ryan in the kitchen I put my thoughts on hold. I placed my bare feet on the cold floor and made my way into the kitchen.

"Hey Ryan, can I make you anything?" I said through my morning voice.

"No, I'm good" he replied in a stern tone.

"Okay, what time do you think you will be home tonight? I was thinking maybe we could go out to eat at Red Robin with Maddy, she loves all the bright lights there and especially loves the french fries"

"Megan, why do you nag me? You know I have a huge case that I have to work on every night. I will be eating dinner at the office and please don't wait up for me" he said while making his coffee. Feeling like someone just punched me, I left the room. *What is the use* I thought, *He will never change. He is too into his work and if I never get time with him, I will never be able to show him how his life is actually really good.*

Frustrated I laid back down on the bed. The cries of Maddy interrupted my thoughts and I walked quickly to her room.

"Mama, Mama, out," Maddy said as she reached for me. Her chubby little arms were up in the air waiting for me to pick her up. As I picked her up, she wrapped her tiny fingers around my hair as she had done for as long as she could control her fingers. It was a habit she had developed, and I didn't mind it, as long as she didn't pull down too hard.

I heard the front door close as I realized Ryan didn't say goodbye to me or Maddy. In fact, he hadn't even seen his daughter today and she would be in bed before he got home.

"This is no way to live," I said aloud. His actions enforced my thought that health does not equal happiness.

Chapter 14

I decided to play on the floor with Maddy. Together we took the large pieces of a puzzle with little knobs on it and created a butterfly. Maddy was growing so quickly, it seemed like she was changing and doing new things daily. It was so sad that Ryan was missing all the precious moments. How could he care more about work than sweet Maddy? When and how did this happen? The Ryan that I married loved spending every moment with me. But now he just cared about working and making money, he had lost sight of the important things in life. My eyes wandered to the mantel as I surveyed the large pale pink conch shell with a hint of a yellow. Just the sight of it brought me back to our honeymoon.

The waves crashed along the Maui shoreline. Ryan and I had just gotten married and flew the next day to Maui. I loved everything to do with the ocean and sandy beaches. Hand in hand we walked towards the turquoise waters that went as far as the eye could see.

"Ry, I hope we see some really beautiful fish today!" I said with excitement as I grabbed my snorkel and mask.

"Me too!" We entered the warm salty water, put our heads under and were instantly transported to the underwater world full of all colors. Large fish and small yellow fish and bright colors of clownfish surrounded us.

Ryan pointed enthusiastically below us. I couldn't believe what I was seeing. About ten feet below I saw something that I first thought was a black snake. Suddenly, I realized it was an electric eel. Quickly we swam away, further into the depths and rainbow sights. We swam and snorkeled for several hours. Time passed as we looked at all the sea creatures.

With wrinkled skin, we finally made our way to the shore. The sun shone on my skin as we approached our towels.

"Ryan, it doesn't get much better than this," I said as I surveyed the beauty surrounding me in all directions.

"I know Megs, life is good. I love you so much" and with that, he leaned over and kissed me gently.

I had never felt so much love and emotion all at once in my life.

"I love you too Ryan. I hope we are always this in love, I hope we never let life or work or kids or anything come between us."

"Megan, you know I love being a lawyer, but it can not hold a candle to how I feel about you. There is no that could ever take me away from you. You are a precious gift that I intend to treasure for all of my days"

Our honeymoon continued with more adventures including a luau, hiking to a waterfall and taking in breathtaking sunsets. On the last day we were there we were in a little beachside souvenir store when I spotted the conch shell.

"Ryan we have to get this," I said picking up the shell and inspecting it from all sides.

I was taken aback by the simple beauty of something that had once made its home underwater. I imagined the snail that used to live in it. Now we would be able to enjoy the unoccupied shell.

We purchased the shell and placed it in our new home. Every time I saw it, it reminded me of the beauty and love of our honeymoon.

Those days seemed a million miles away now. I hardly recognized the Ryan I had been living with. I wished he would look into my eyes the way he used to, I wished he would for once see me. It was an awful feeling to be invisible, to feel like my very existence did not matter. I remember feeling the same way after my dad died. We were surrounded by so many friends and family when he was sick and also right after he died. People were there for us as we adjusted to the new normal of having a family of four instead of five. For about two months people would bring over casseroles and meatloaves and all sorts of meals. As a child I never really understood why people brought us meals. *Do they think this will bring my dad back* I would often think. How could food make us better? Being a picky eater, I really didn't like what people brought. Each time a hot casserole was brought to our front door I wondered how it would help with the hole I was feeling in my heart. How could tater tots and beef ease the pain of losing my dad way too soon?

A few months after my dad passed away the meals came less often. The constant flow of people coming into our house began to get more sporadic. My friends at school didn't know how to act around me. When I had first returned to school, I had a few friends who asked how I was but for the most part, they pretended like nothing happened. Their world continued when mine had stopped. And when I say stopped, I mean in my bed with the covers over my head, hoping I would die. I used to stay under my covers for hours and cry until there were no more tears left to cry. I would pray for the pain to stop, pray for time to be reversed and scream out to God for taking away my daddy.

In those days I too felt invisible. Invisible to those around me whose lives continued on. Invisible to my mom who was dealing with her own grief and invisible in my pain. So being invisible to Ryan brought back painful memories that I had tried to bury deep inside under all the layers of pain I tried to hide over the years.

What should I do? My mind had still been pondering ways to help Ryan understand how good he had it but I still hadn't come up with a very good solution, not for lack of trying. He seemed so distant and unreachable. I wished I could read his thoughts and know what he was thinking. In order to move forward, I would have to first know more of where he was at. I planned to question him when he got home. Even though Ryan told me not to wait up for him I could not wait another day to talk to him about what was happening in his mind. Engrossed in a reality show I was watching I didn't hear Ryan's truck approaching the house. The front door opened, and I paused my show. Ryan walked into the room.

"You can turn the light on, I am not sleeping," I said.

Without even speaking a word to me Ryan loosened his tie and started getting ready for bed.

"Ryan, we need to talk," I said.

"Okay," he replied hesitantly.

"Ryan, I need to know more about what is making you so unhappy, you know Ryan, life could be so much worse! What would you think if you were paralyzed? Would you think work would matter so much then? When was the last time you played with Maddy? Do you even know how many words she says now?"

"Whoah, why are you attacking me?"

"Ryan, I am not attacking you, I am just trying to understand you"

"Why are you asking me about being paralyzed? That is a strange question!" he said as he raised his eyebrows.

"I just know that life can change in an instant and things could always be worse. We both have our health and I have always heard it said that if money can't fix it, it's not a problem, meaning we have our health so we really have nothing, nada, to complain about."

"Megan, I think being home alone is messing with your mind. I get what you're saying but you are acting a little crazy, I do love Maddy and I spend time with her, I want to spend more time with her but someone has to make money around here!" he said as he stormed out of the room.

I was getting nowhere with this. Recalling my conversation with my dad in heaven I realized he was right; you cannot change people. It was no use. If I was going to live with him, he would just continue to be unhappy.

If I was living with paralyzed Ryan, he wouldn't have his health but at least he would have his happiness, or more accurately his joy. I realized that I couldn't have the happy, healthy Ryan I had dreamed of. I had to pick.one or the other. The more I thought about it the harder it became.

In life what was more important happiness or health? I could either have a husband who was paralyzed with joy or a husband who had paralyzed joy but a healthy body. There was no easy choice, no simple follow the line's decision. No clear cut answers. Somehow, I had to decide. I was never told how much time I would get to decide but I wanted to be prepared for when I had to make a choice. I hated that I had to decide but was also happy that I was given the rare gift of seeing two lives. People didn't usually get this choice. Although it was nearly impossible to decide I knew I was so blessed to be in the position of having to choose. What if I only knew one Ryan and never knew how full of joy he could be? As I looked around my room, I decided to close my eyes, let sleep take me away and worry about tomorrow at another time. God even tells us to not worry about tomorrow, and with that, I rested my mind, body, and soul and drifted off to sleep.

Chapter 15

Sleep quickly overtook me and when I woke up I was amidst the field of tulips yet again. This has been quite the journey traveling back and forth between heaven and earth as well as traveling between healthy and paralyzed Ryan. I felt like my life was in an emotional blender at all times. I never knew what the day may hold or how I would feel.

As I stood up and surveyed the intensity of yellow tulips as far as I could see I wondered what would happen this trip to heaven. Each time I was in heaven it felt a little more like home and I wanted to stay longer. Every time I would experience a peace that could not be explained, and it made me want to linger. I wanted to have that peace forever and never go back to the pain I knew awaited me on earth.

Either life I chose, there would be pain and heartache. Both lives would include suffering as I comprehended more every day that the world was not my home. I also wondered if I would get to see more of heaven than just the tulips. What was beyond the fields? Would I meet the one behind the voice? Would I meet my savior, the one who paid the ultimate price for me to be in heaven?

I took a deep breath and breathed in the pure air of heaven that invaded my lungs and filled me with a calm that exceeded anything I had ever known before.

"Can I just stay here?" I said aloud. As if my words had been heard a butterfly began to fly above my head. The wings were brighter shades of color than I had ever known. I understood the symbolism of the butterfly at this exact moment. A butterfly represents rebirth, transformation, a chance to become something new. I knew the gift of seeing my life play out in two different ways was a chance to grow and turn into the woman I was created to be, I also understood that with great privilege comes great responsibility. This choice, though a gift was weighing heavily upon me.

In the far distance, barely visible I could make out the outlines of a group of people. I decided to walk towards them as I didn't know what else I was supposed to be doing this trip to heaven. As I started walking towards them, I was suddenly right in front of them in what seemed to be only a second for me. I took in the scene before me. There were about ten people gathered around a large, rectangular table with a white tablecloth. Giant platters of all kinds of food adorned the plates and large glasses were filled to the brim with a bright blue colored liquid.

"Megan!" I heard several voices say in unison.

Confused, I looked around the table. No one appeared to be past their mid-twenties and in addition, there were two children around four or five years old sitting at the table.

I was so confused as to why they were saying my name especially when I didn't recognize any of them.

"Hi," I said hesitantly "Do, do I know you?"

Laughter filled the air and the joy they carried was infectious. I didn't know how they knew me, but I wanted to be a part of their fun.

"Megan, you may not know us, but we all know you, each one of us has been affected by your life and Ryan's life in some way. You are here today to listen as we share how your life has impacted us in a multitude of ways.

The concept interested me.

"Here, please sit." A smiling man said as he motioned to the chair at the head of the table. I slowly sat down and turned my attention to the woman who began speaking.

"Megan, my name is Cheyanne, I know I don't look like it but I am 92 years old, well at least I was until I left earth for this place" she said motioning in all directions. "Your life affected me even though you never knew it, my son Charlie was paralyzed. He was newly paralyzed

113

after a swimming accident. Anyways, he has a mutual friend with you who shared your video when you said "If God allowed it, I can accept it. Megan, those words changed my boys' life. He was so angry at one point; he was living in a marinade of sadness and self-pity but what you said in that video changed the direction of his life. He realized he had something to live for and started trying to find joy in everyday life. He stopped complaining and started embracing life. He was able to share with me before I entered heaven that he was a changed person, accepting his paralyzed body he could also accept my death. Thank you for helping my boy," she said.

"I want to share; I want to share" A little hand waved in the air. A little girl with golden curls, dimples and a huge smile looked at me.

"Yes, what do you want to share?"

"My mom met you once at church. You prayed for her and for me. She told you about my cancer and how sick I was feeling and you prayed with her. Your Ryan had just been paralyzed and you were going to have a baby and you still made time to pray with us. You told my mom "I may not understand, but something that has helped me is knowing that if God allowed it, I can accept it." My mama came home and rocked me to sleep. I never woke up from that sleep on earth, I woke up here, and this is the best place ever! Thank you for helping my mom when I was sick and when I went to heaven."

"You are welcome sweetie." My mind was spinning from the words just spoken to me. How could it be that during the darkest times when I was at my lowest when I was at my worst that God has used me in other lives? I remember the days of when Ryan was first paralyzed and I was in survival mode, I was just barely keeping my head above water. I had no idea that God was using me so much in the lives of others. It reminded me again that when we are reliant only on God, not on a person, substance or anything else, then we are void of our own selfishness and God can fill us and use us more mightily than ever. He can do things that we never thought possible. I can see now how my life had touched those around the table.

A young man with dark hair stood up.

"Megan, we have never met, but you are a huge part of why I am in heaven today"

I studied the man intently; I could not believe that a man I never met would say I was a huge part of him being in heaven.

"My wife Anne and I- well I believe you know her from college, well we were having some major problems in our marriage, in fact, she told me that she was getting ready to leave me when she saw something you posted online. It was something about how God chose you to be by your husband's side during his accident. How God had specifically picked you. That made my wife think about being married to me. She contemplated that she was chosen to be my wife. That despite all of our troubles, she had committed to me and was chosen to be my wife.

That day instead of being critical and threatening to leave me she started just loving me. She started loving me unconditionally. I know it was really hard on her. And as she loved me, my heart began to soften. Through a series of events, I was able to get to know her faith. I used to always just make fun of her when she left for church but then I started going with her, and when I went with her I learned where her hope and peace came from. I realized that I was a sinner and without Jesus, I was lost.

I asked Jesus to forgive me and come into my heart. That day I became a new man, Unfortunately, for my friends and family the next day I was in a car accident. I died instantly and awoke here. I love that my wife and kids know where I am, and you Megan Montgomery played a role in all of this, your life has touched more lives than you understand."

Tears formed in my eyes as I recalled my friend Anne who was on my soccer team in college. We were never very close but had stayed in touch via social media. I recalled seeing that her husband had passed away, but I never had any idea that I had any impact on his life whatsoever. Such a sobering fact to realize that my actions impacted so much more than I realized. Each decision though it may seem small at the time can have an eternal impact. I so wished more people on earth understood this concept. If people did, they would be much more careful about their actions, what a privilege that I was able to meet some of the people my life had impacted up until this point.

A woman with long, straight black hair stood up. "Megan I am so happy to see you again. I am another life you touched where you had no idea. I was at the rehabilitation clinic at the same time as your Ryan. You met me, but I looked so different at that time that I am sure you don't recognize me. I heard you ask a nurse about me one day and she told you I had no one that visited me. I wasn't married and didn't have kids or parents. I also had no friends as I wasn't the nicest person to be around. Like your husband, I was in a car accident and also became instantly paralyzed, by the time I was at the clinic I was in a dark depression. You walked into my room and started talking to me. At first, I wasn't very receptive to talking to you and ignored your kindness, but you never gave up.

Day after day you stopped by to share an encouraging word or verse. You taped verses to the ceiling so I could see them. With no sign that I was getting anything out of your visits you continued day after day, you told me that Jesus loved me and to never give up. You told me how to ask him to be part of my life, but I wasn't ready. You said goodbye on the day Ryan left but that isn't where my story ends. One day a chaplain who visited the clinic came to my room. He saw the verses you had taped up and started a conversation about them. Because of your love, my heart was open to learning more. I asked Jesus into my life that day. If you would not have loved me even through your pain, I don't think I would be here today. You were instrumental to me being here. The day after the chaplain came, I died from an infection and complications. I want to thank you for loving me"

"Yes, I remember you, it's Jenny, right?" I said as I got up from my chair and made my way towards her. I wrapped my arms around her tightly in a hug. "Jenny thank you for sharing with me the impact I had on your life, I had no idea"

It was all so overwhelming in a good way to see the lives I impacted. Suddenly it hit me that all of the stories I heard were from my life when Ryan was paralyzed If I went back to the life I was living now none of these stories would happen. I realized that this decision was so much more than just my life. I realized it had a ripple effect big enough to start a tsunami. And with the realization of the tsunami-sized decision to make I sat down to ponder it all.

Chapter 16

Sitting at the table surrounded by people that my life with Ryan had touched I was overwhelmed by the impact my little life had had. One of the lies I had believed was that I was unimportant, that I didn't matter and that no one cared. The last lie was oftentimes the strongest and most deeply felt. When Ryan was in his accident people swarmed to help, or so it seemed.

Sometimes I felt like people cared more about what was going on so they could gossip about it. Regardless of whether that was true or not the enemy used the lie that I was alone in my pain to really get to me. In those moments when the house was quiet and there was no one around to see me on the floor crying or hear my heart break into a thousand pieces as the dream, I dreamed for myself and my future family crumbled in front of me I felt utterly alone in my pain. Yes, the logical part of me knew that people cared but the emotional side of me many times didn't and thus I felt alone.

If I put my emotions away and looked at things from a rational perspective, I could see that my life was overflowing with people who cared who didn't always know how to show me or know what to do. The enemy knew my triggers and ways to get to me. In my resolve to consider all my trials pure joy I often felt attacked and suddenly weak. When I was weak, I was less effective at helping those around me, thus the attacks on my heart.

As though a layer of fog was lifted from my eyes I became aware of how important and instrumental I was in God's plan for not only my life and my family's life but the lives of others that I may or may not know. The ripple effect of my life showed me that my trials and finding joy in them were a huge blessing and responsibility. My emotions had been all over the place during this whole process. I thought in the beginning that I knew the answers, I thought I knew the best plan for my life, but going between paralyzed and healthy Ryan I realized I actually didn't know what was best for my life. Yes, this was a rare gift to be given the chance to see two versions of my life but also a huge responsibility. Now that I had learned of the lives that had been touched how could I go back knowing that these lives wouldn't have been changed in the same ways?

I excused myself from the table and walked towards the vibrant yellow tulips which were still spread in every direction that I looked. I knew what I needed to do, I needed to get away to pray and clear my head, to communicate with the only one who was in fact always there for me. The one who did see every tear and every time my heart broke. The one who was able to hold me tight and at the same time allow me to be my own person.

I looked up into the piercing blue sky

"Oh Jesus, I need your help," I said.

At that moment the most amazing thing I had ever experienced happened. To my right appeared a light with greater intensity than I had ever known. Under the light, I could see a man. The light was bright, and it was hard to see details, but I could see kind eyes and a smiling face. Without even stopping to think I knew it must be Jesus. In all my trips to heaven, I had never had the privilege of meeting Jesus face to face. Instantly I fell to my knees. All through my life in the happiest times and darkest times I had imagined this moment. The time I remember picturing this the most was right after my dad died. As I cried 10-year-old broken heart tears for the loss of my daddy I would imagine what it would be like to meet Jesus and here I was.

"Megan, I love you, I know you have heard that all of your life, but I want you to really grasp it, to comprehend it and to know that you are important, you are special and you are my daughter."

I was now looking directly into the face of Jesus. His eyes were so kind. The way he looked at me was unlike anything I had ever experienced before. The closest thing I could compare it to was looking into my daddy's eyes. A flood of emotions overtook me. How could it be possible to be staring into my savior's face? The peaceful feeling I had had every time I was in heaven intensified while standing next to Jesus. He knew every single thing about me. All of it. Every single ugly hidden thing and yet he loved me. He knew my secret thoughts and all of my insecurities and yet he loved me. He knew the times I had walked away from him, denying him with my life, yet he still loved me. Tears streaming down my face I replied

"Thank you for loving me, thank you for forgiving me and thank you for this gift you are giving me. I know what I need to do, but it means laying down what I really want."

"Yes, child, it does. But I promise you that I love and care for you so much that I do have a plan, you just have to trust me. There will be times when you don't feel like I do, but I promise I will always make beauty from ashes and I do see every tear." With that millions of glass bottles appeared in the field of tulips. There was a string and a colored piece of paper hanging off every one of them. There was every shade of colors and some colors I had never seen. Written in beautiful calligraphy letters were names. I looked to my feet to the row in front of me. Carefully written were the words Megan Montgomery.

"Precious child, these are your tears"

I stared in disbelief as I began walking down the row. Bottle after bottle was filled to the rim with a clear liquid that I knew must be my tears. Every jar in the row for as far as I could see had my name on it. Touched by this act I was utterly speechless. I had never known such love. Sure, I had always believed in God's love since my Sunday school days of singing "Jesus loves me" but I had never really truly understood the depths of his love.

To actually carefully wipe my tears and save them in a bottle was more than my mind could comprehend. Jesus walked to one of the bottles near the beginning of the row and carefully picked it up. "This one was from when you were new at school and didn't have any friends. You went into the bathroom at recess and cried, you thought you were alone, but I was there and saved your tears." He continued walking a few bottles down the row. "These" he said as he picked up a handful of bottles, "were from when your father died, some of these tears people saw, but the majority of them were from when you were alone at night in your bed. I was there right beside you, wiping your tears and collecting them here" he kept walking

124

"This one was from when your best friend in college decided to walk away from you and you felt betrayed. I know you felt even more alone in this pain because it was hard to talk about with others and you didn't want to make a big deal about it, but Megan, I was there, I felt your pain and saw your tears, even if no one else did." He continued walking farther down the row.

He picked up more bottles, "And these Megan are from when Ryan was in the accident, these tears fill many jars as it has been one of your most devastating times. I know that in the pain of watching your dreams crumble you feel so alone, so very alone. But Megan, don't listen to the lies of the enemy. You are never alone, you got that? Never, ever, ever. Often times I even send my people to do my work. The friend that calls you out of the blue? That's me, the meal dropped off at your house? Me and many other ways. So please, when the enemy tries to make you feel alone, remember all the people I have put into your life and also, please remember this moment, this visual of how much I love you. Megan, I just want you to get it, I love you so much! I want to spend time with you every second of every day. Sometimes on the days, you are feeling alone I will put people and my word in front of you to remind you and sometimes you don't even notice.

125

Sometimes you let the lies of the enemy cloud and skew what is really going on. Megan don't buy into those lies anymore. He will try to get you down because he wants to see you feel sorry for yourself and become ineffective. Megan, He wants to steal your joy my love."

The gravity of the words that he spoke to me filled my mind. He was so right, he had always been there for me, every single day of my life. Why had I let the enemy lie to me so many times? Why had I let him trick me into thinking I was all alone in my pain? That was such an immense lie that I wanted to fight it with every fiber in my being. I knew that if I was feeling this way that so many more people must also struggle with feeling alone.

I wanted to go back and do God's work so others might not feel so alone and let Him use me to help those who were struggling. I wished I had my phone with me so I could take a picture of the endless rows of bottles of tears. I wanted everyone to know that Jesus actually saves their tears in a bottle, that he is actually there with them and there really is a place that He keeps them.

Suddenly I knew what I had to do, I had to go back to paralyzed Ryan and help him and others. I needed to shift life from being about what I wanted to being about what God wanted and how and where he could best use me. I no longer wanted to be consumed by paralyzed joy.

Chapter 17

After talking to Jesus I knew what I needed to do. The rows of tears in a bottle had overwhelmed me in a good way. The evidence of his love was so extraordinarily strong. The bottles in front of me vanished as well as Jesus. Still thankful for my time with Jesus I walked back towards the table of people. My mind was made up, I must return once and for all to my life with paralyzed Ryan. I knew it would be extremely difficult, but I also knew it was the best for me and all involved. As I walked through the row of tulips, I suddenly felt sleepy. I laid down and fell fast asleep with an unexplainable peace overtaking me.

"Mama, mama, mama" a sweet little voice awakened me.

I sat up suddenly and realized I was home and that was the cry of my Maddy. As my feet touched the cold floor, I realized I was stepping into my destiny and my purpose. Approaching Maddy's crib her infectious smile was staring at me. She had her arms straight up in the air

"Out mama, out."

I picked her up and she rubbed her face against me and snuggled in. There was nothing in the world quite as sweet as my baby girl in the morning. I changed her diaper and dressed her in fresh clothes. Maddy was getting bigger, she was now eighteen months and not just walking, but running everywhere. I set her on the ground and she ran out of the room. I knew she was going to see her favorite person in the world, her daddy.

"Dada, dada" she said while running down the hall. Her little legs ran as fast as they could to reach him. I knew that because he had a smaller range of motion than before he could hear the sweet sounds of Maddy approaching. I followed her into the room as she looked at me with arms straight up and said,

"Up Dada" I knew what she wanted me to do. I picked her up and set her on his stomach. This was something they both loved. Her chubby little fingers grabbed his cheeks and he laughed. I loved watching the bond between them. Maddy had never known her dad any differently than how he was now. He was her hero and Ryan thought Maddy was a princess who could do no wrong. Seeing the bond between them it confirmed that I had, in fact, made the right choice.

In this life, Ryan had so much more time with his family. It may not have been the kind of time I dreamed of when I walked down the aisle to him, but it was my new dream.

"Princess, I love you so much," Ryan said to Maddy who was still sitting on his stomach. I stayed near to make sure she didn't fall off as had almost happened a few times. I heard the doorbell and knew it must be one of Ryan's nurses. I put Maddy down and she ran behind me to run toward the door. I opened up the door and was surprised to see my mom instead of his nurse.

"Mom, what are you doing here?"

"Can't a mom just come to visit her daughter and granddaughter?" Maddy squeezed past me and squealed

"Nana!" I was so thankful that my mom had never left the area and then even when I left for college I eventually moved back home. After my dad died, we were extremely close as we weathered the grief process as well. My brothers had grieved in other ways. I had two older brothers, Alex and Mike and they also had stayed in the area. I used to get so angry at them that they rarely cried over my dad being gone, sometimes it appeared that they didn't even care.

Alex tried to stay busy and was rarely home, he seemed to be gone constantly with friends or with different girlfriends that came and went. He was four years older than me, so I know things were a lot different for him as a fourteen-year-old boy than for me as a ten-year-old girl. Fourteen was already such a strange, awkward stage, then adding the death of his father it was a really hard time for Alex. He struggled with what to do with his emotions, often late at night, I would see him outside my window jumping on our large trampoline. He was yelling as he jumped, I usually couldn't figure out what he was saying but I knew he was dealing with his anger. My mom always said his jumping on the trampoline was better than him punching someone, so she allowed it even when it was late at night. When we were young, we weren't very close I believe mostly due to our vastly different stages and ages but over the years we had grown closer. He had become a protective brother who always had my back and I know him seeing Ryan paralyzed was hard for him.

My brother Mike was more quiet and reserved. Sometimes he didn't even seem to have an emotional bone in his body. I remember the days following my father's death and even at my father's funeral he didn't shed a tear, or at least never in front of anyone. He seemed to lock his emotions up tightly as if he were afraid to let them out of his sight for fear of losing control. My mind began to wander back to my father's funeral.

My father was a huge college football fan and before his death he told my mom that he didn't want his funeral to be full of boring black clothes, but instead, he wanted people to wear their favorite sports team gear. The church was bright with so many colors in all directions as people filed in wearing their favorite sports team shirts, hats and more. It was unlike any funeral I had ever seen or heard of. I remember that day feeling like a dream. So surreal, I just knew it couldn't be true. But my daddy's lifeless body in the open casket at the front of the church told me otherwise.

I know my mom had struggled on whether his body should be there or not, but she thought it would help us kids to say goodbye. I stared at his body in shock. I had already said goodbye to him at the hospital. This body in front of me was not my dad. His soul was missing, and the body didn't even look like him. I could tell make-up had been applied to his face and that is something he would never do. The near five hundred guests filed into the sanctuary of our church as person after person hugged me and said, "I'm so sorry".

I felt numb, I didn't know how to feel, and this was all too much for my little mind to comprehend. I heard soft music in the background as a video of my dad started to play on the large screen in front of the church. Pictures starting from when he was a baby filled the screen. With each passing picture, I felt the dam holding back my tears become closer to breaking. I had not wanted to cry but the weight of the event happening was too much. When the picture of daddy holding me on the day I was born flashed on the screen, the tears cascaded uncontrollably down my face.

"This isn't fair God!" I thought as I continued to watch the pictures of my family across the screen. Picture after picture seemed to throw daggers into my inner being. The pictures stopped and a video of my dad started playing. Seeing my dad on the screen and my dad's body in front of me was too much. I felt the arms of my grandmother on my back.

"It's okay sweet Megan, let it all out, it's okay."

I looked up from the ground and saw my father on the screen. He was dancing with my mom on their wedding day, full of youth and smiles he looked so full of life, so vibrant and I knew he must be like this again in heaven, the video turned into us cutting down a Christmas tree, something we had done for as long as I could remember. It was always one of my favorite family memories, my dad looked so strong and young in the video, I stood up again and let my grandmother's arms wrap around me. The Christmas tree video was gone and turned to one of my favorite memories of my dad in his last year of life, my family

133

was at one of his favorite college sports teams football games and during a time out the song, Shout came on and he started singing it and dancing with my brothers and I, it was one of the last trips we ever took with him then in one last video we were at Disneyland and he was riding a scooter in front of Sleeping Beauty's castle in Disneyland, he lifted up his hands and said " I made it world, I made it" and with that, the video was over.

I looked around and every single person I saw was crying. I knew it was my turn to go to the stage, my mom had told me I didn't have to do it but I told her I really wanted to.
Wearing my Dad's green and yellow college shirt I made my way to the stage. There was not a dry eye in the place, and I knew when I started singing they would cry again.
"This one's for you daddy," I said into the microphone.

The familiar song that my dad had sung for me since I was born began to play on the loudspeakers. Through a wobbly voice, I began singing "You are my sunshine, my only sunshine, you make me happy when skies are gray" Tears freely flowing I continued. "You'll never know daddy how much I love you, please don't take my sunshine away" and with that I fell to the floor.

Chapter 18

My thoughts returned to the present reality. Though my dad's death was a long time ago, it still felt recent in many ways. I returned to talking to my mother who had come to visit me. My mother was now on the floor playing blocks with Maddy. I loved watching the two of them play. They had huge smiles on their faces and Maddy kept letting out little giggles.

"Did you come over to see me or Maddy?" I asked.

" Haha, I came to see both of you, and how is Ryan today?"

"He is still asleep; I will check on him in a little bit."

They continued playing for a while.

"Mom, how did you do it?" I asked suddenly.

"Do what?" she looked at me inquisitively.

"How did you keep such a positive attitude when dad died and how did you manage to be a single parent? I know Ryan is still here, but it feels like I am a single parent since he can't help with anything and oftentimes I look at my friends and their happy, healthy families and honestly mom I feel jealous. I wonder why it can't be me and Maddy and healthy Ryan?"

Like a ton of bricks, I realized what I had said. I actually had experienced that exact scenario and it was not what I had wanted. In that scenario, my Ryan was not happy. The words were already out of my mouth and I was interested in how my mom would reply.

"Oh Megan, things were not always as you assumed they were, You know as a mother you try to shield your children from pain. I did that same thing for you and your brothers. You didn't see all the nights that I cried myself to sleep, you didn't see the tearful conversations I had with my friends. I did my best to hold it together for you three. Right after your father died, I felt like I might die right along with him. I don't think you knew it but I fought depression and suicide. You kids and the peace of God are what kept me here."

I was shocked as my mom continued

"The biggest thing that helped me was staying plugged into a Christ-centered community. The enemy wants us to feel alone and if I would have given up going to church and Bible study that is what would have happened. I would have been alone in my pain. It was hard at first. I mean my whole identity changed. I was married to your dad for nearly 20 years and suddenly I was single again? Talk about a strange feeling! Not only did I connect at church, but I found a Christian support group for widows and they were the lifeline that God gave me during this time.

They had walked this road before me and could help me through the process of learning my new normal. They had all lost their husbands. They lost their husbands in various ways and at different ages but we all had one thing in common, knowing the sting of the death of a spouse. The ones I could relate to the most had children. For me, sweet Megan, watching you guys suffer was harder than my own pain. It was hard even before he died. I learned of something called anticipatory grief. This is where you know a loved one is going to die and it feels like you are on a train track and you know the train is going to hit you, there is absolutely nothing you can do to stop it. You wake up each day knowing its closer and wondering if today is the day it will hit you. Well for me, the image I had in my head was you and your brothers on the track. I knew the train was headed for you but there was absolutely nothing I could do to stop it. Imagine a train coming at Maddy, you would desperately try to stop it, to ease her pain, but you couldn't."

Her last words sunk deep into my soul. I had never thought about things that way. Now, as a mother, I could understand how my

137

mom must have felt. I could understand the immensity of the burden she carried for me and my brothers.

She continued, "When I realized there was no way for me to stop the train I began to plead and beg God to at least soften the blow of the train. I knew that it was indeed going to hit you, I knew that you indeed were going to be hurt, but I prayed desperately that God would make the pain less, that he would ease the pain of the inevitable. Even when we knew he only had a few months, even a few weeks from dying we prayed for a miracle. Do you remember that?" She said looking in my direction.

"Yes, every night I would say "God, I know you can heal my daddy, I know you have the power, I ask for a complete miracle for him, and God please let that healing be here on earth"

My mom's eyes welled up with tears as she softly spoke again.

"Yes, we all prayed that. We had people telling us all kinds of things. I even had a woman I didn't know call and tell me that I needed to just believe, and he would be healed, that it was only unbelief that would cause him not to be healed. She actually told me to tell you that your father would for sure be healed on earth. Megan, could you imagine what that would be like if I had told you that? As much as I wanted it to be true that he would be healed, I knew that if I told you that and we didn't get a miraculous healing on earth that you would question God and maybe even walk away from him. I feel like for the most part, people meant well, but oftentimes our earthly mind can't understand God's heavenly ways, so people give the wrong information.

You asked about how I was able to stay so positive, well I clung to the promises of God. Did you know that there are over 5,000 of them? The enemy will try his best to get us to not believe them, but I was determined to get to know the promises and memorize many of them so in my sad times, my lonely and vulnerable times I could pull them out, I learned that the battle belongs to the Lord. I need to be equipped and ready, but ultimately, he would fight it for me.

"Megan, I still take such comfort in knowing God is always by my side, always. Even when I went from sleeping beside my husband for nearly 20 years to sleeping alone in my bed. Even when people who didn't know my story would ask about my husband and I would have to relive the pain all over again. I love the verse about how God takes our yoke upon him. .Matthew 11:28-30 *"Come to me, all you who are weary and burdened, and I will give you rest. [29] Take my yoke upon you and learn from me, for I am gentle and humble in heart, and you will find rest for your souls. [30] For my yoke is easy and my burden is light."*

"Megan, I especially love that one for the visual it gives me. A yoke was used for animals like an ox and they would carry the burden and the load together, I loved picturing God taking my heavy burden off of me so I could rest. He did too, so many times when I felt I couldn't keep going he would provide some way for me to receive rest, from providing someone to take you kids so I could take a nap or a bubble bath to the nights when I was too exhausted to make dinner and someone would bring a meal to the times when I could simply cry in God's arms and feel an unexplainable peace that can only be found in His arms."

I loved learning these pieces of wisdom from my mother. My mother exuded such grace and wisdom and I hoped I could be like her as I continued living my difficult life with a paralyzed husband.

My mother continued, "There are so many promises that have meant so much to me, especially when I became a widow.

"Megan, I held and still hold onto those promises so tightly. I let the wise words of wisdom from my mother sink in.

"Thank you, mom, for sharing with me the way you have persevered through your hardest times. I have learned that no one's life turns out exactly how they thought it would. I have learned that everyone has a story. Every single person. If they don't admit it, they still have things that aren't as they thought it would be. But the key to joy is embracing the life given to you at the moment you are in. Not looking too far back and not looking too far into the future. I have learned to be content in each minute that God gifts me, every single day,"

My mother wiped away the tears that had formed on her face as she kissed Maddy on the top of her head. Looking at the two girls in front of me I felt such joy and peace.

Chapter 19

Shortly after my mother sharing with me, I heard the distinct tone in my phone that meant that Ryan needed me. Ryan had an iPad that he could use a pen with to open apps and call for me.

"Just a minute mom, I'll be back in a few."

"Take your time I'll keep playing with this little angel," she said while touching the top of Maddy's head.

"Coming," I said as I stood up and headed towards Ryan's room.

Sometimes it made me sad to recall that his room used to be our room. His hospital-style bed was bulky and loud and although I had tried to stay in the room several times I always ended up too exhausted to be any good to anyone the next day and together we agreed that I should move the bed Ryan and I used to share to down the hall in the guest room. I was used to sleeping alone, I was still up every few hours first peeking in on Maddy and then looking in on him.

I had grown accustomed to our new way of life and I hardly remembered what it was like to share a bed with my husband. As a newlywed that in itself was a lot to get used to, I had come to understand that we would never be intimate again. Sometimes that fact broke my heart as the images of my future children disappeared before my eyes. I knew that adoption could be considered but knowing that I would be caring for Ryan the rest of my life made that thought not much of a possibility. My future was not what I dreamed of, but I was making the best of it.

I walked into what was now a usual site, Ryan in his hospital bed eyes pointed at the ceiling. I was thankful that my brother Alex had come over and installed a tv on the ceiling which helped Ryan pass the time. I had often thought about how awful it would be to be trapped in Ryan's body unable to move, just passing time and relying on others for my every need. Ryan's attitude could be a lot worse but despite his circumstances, he kept himself in surprisingly good spirits.

"Hi baby," I said. As he turned his head to see me.

His deep brown eyes still took my breath away. I was so thankful that he had his full memory, I imagined how much harder this would be if he didn't even know me.

"Hi, Megs, good morning. I was wondering if you could read to me. I know I could listen to books being read to me, but it is soothing to me to hear you read."

"Sure, just let me make sure my mom can keep watching Maddy for a little while."

I returned a few moments later and just as I had thought it was not a problem for my mom at all to watch Maddy. She absolutely loved watching Maddy and was a godsend to me when I was caring for Ryan.

"What do you want me to read to you?" I asked looking at the row of books on our bookshelf. We had all kinds of books, the biggest category being Christian non-fiction.

"How about the Bible? Sometimes I feel like it's best to hear straight from God rather than opinions and thoughts about Him, I want to hear from Him. I am feeling weak today. Megs it's a hard day" and with that, a single tear fell down his cheek. I wiped it with a nearby Kleenex and was instantly reminded of the vision of Jesus in heaven with all of my tears. I decided to look up that verse and the verses that followed and read them to him.

I decided to read it in the New Living Translation this time, I often changed up which version I read the bible in as each one helped me understand it in a little different way. I sat down in the chair next to Ryan.

"These verses have meant a lot to me recently, especially the ones about our tears in a bottle, I hope it helps you too.

"You keep track of all my sorrows. You have collected all my tears in your bottle. You have recorded each one in your book." Psalm 56:8

I stopped reading and looked over at Ryan. He seemed to be deep in thought.

"What are you thinking," I said as I swept his hair to the side.

"Just how much God loves me and just as it says near the end, he has rescued me from death. Also, I need to keep trusting God. So often I get lost in my own self-pity that I forget how much God has helped me. I could have died instantly in the car accident Megan. Or as a vegetable for years, not in heaven but not really here? I already feel as if I am a total burden to you but what if it was worse and you couldn't even talk to me? What then? Megs I am so proud of you, I know I don't say it very often but so many other women would have left, but you have stayed by my side even though I know this was not your plan. Oh, Megan, I wish I could give you the life we dreamed of, I wish I could give you more kids and travel with you and all the things we used to dream about." we can still dream and God will help us realize those dreams.

"Ryan, it's okay. Maybe this isn't what we dreamed of and again I don't think God caused this to happen but he did allow it so I know it's part of his plan and his plan isn't that you would go through this alone, he put us together before the accident. He knew we would need each other. Sure, I never dreamed I would be married to a husband who is paralyzed but God has given me the strength minute by minute to be what you need me to be. Ryan, did you know that each day I say "God please give me my manna for today?"

He shook his head no. "What do you mean?"

"Well remember how the Israelites were wandering in the desert for forty years trying to find the promised land? Well, each day God would provide a kind of food called manna. They were told by God to collect just enough for the day. If they saved more than they would eat in a day, it would spoil and get worms in it. If they didn't collect it at all then they would not have anything to eat for the day. So you see, they began to rely on God giving them manna every day, he knew exactly what they needed for that day and he always provided it for them. He does the same thing for me every single day. My manna may come in the form of a friend calling me out of the blue, or you know all those times we have received anonymous checks in the mail? That is God using people to send us Manna. Or sometimes it is a verse I read. But I am telling you Ryan, the manna always comes. The manna increases my faith daily as I know God will always come through."

"I love that Megan, thank you for sharing. I am going to start looking for my manna. Today I believe you are my manna." He said with his smile. I was so thankful that he still had his smile.

"Thank you, my love," I said as I kissed him on his forehead. and he could understand the love behind it.

I shut the Bible and returned to my mother and Maddy.

"Looks like you two have been having fun," I said looking at the toys strewn all over the living room floor.

"Yes, we have" my mother replied.

"Mom, sometimes I feel so helpless watching him in emotional and physical pain and there is absolutely nothing I can do, did you ever feel that way with daddy and his cancer pain?

"Oh yes Megan, many, many times. It was the most heart wrenching thing I had ever experienced. Do you remember towards the end of life he would cry a lot?"

The memories came flooding over me, "How could I forget, I know he tried to hide it from us kids, but I know he was sad a lot."

"Yes, he was. When I married your father, he was so strong, stoic and almost non-emotional. It took a lot to get a tear out of him. In fact, I think we were married for at least five years before I ever saw him cry. He prided himself on being a very private, and unemotional man. Then

147

cancer came. At first, he just cried at the diagnosis. Then the treatment began and when he was hurled over, throwing up I could hear him cry, but still, he didn't cry in front of me. As you know we continued the treatments for a few years and despite our best efforts the tumors still grew. The first time he cried in front of me was the day we decided to stop treatment.

The Dr. had said that most people in his place decide that it wasn't worth the sickness of treatment to possibly extend their life a little longer. I agreed with your father. The day we called the Dr, to tell him was the day that I saw a crack in his armor of defending his emotions. I remember watching his body begin to shake as he let the tears out and said two words over and over.

The words were "Why God, Why God?" I wiped his tears and held him tight. I just let him be emotional and didn't say anything. Sometimes I think it is best to let the ones we love process things in their own time and not try to fix them and make it better. It is time to let them work it out with God, he is actually the only one who can really heal their hearts. After he stopped treatment his pain increased. It wasn't only his physical pain, but his emotional pain. The man who never cried began to cry every day. Sometimes I asked him about it and other times I just let him be. The few times he opened up to me about what he was feeling he said he didn't want to leave me or you kids. I couldn't blame him. I mean Megan can you imagine knowing you would have to leave Ryan and knowing Maddy would grow up without you?"

I silently shook my head from side to side.

"I mean as a parent it is one of the hardest things to face. The tears flowed at night and in the day. I know you saw them, he stopped trying to hide him. Megan, that was when I had to let go. I don't mean let go like give up hope, but I had to let go of trying to emotionally save him and make him happy. I had to stop acting crazy in an attempt to cheer him up. I had to release his emotions to God. I had to do the best I could to carry on every day for you kids, but let go of trying to make him happy every minute. It wasn't working and it wasn't my job. My job was to love him the best I could. I would ask myself each day: How can I be the best wife possible and do you remember what I asked you to ask yourself?"

"Yes," I replied, "How can I be the best daughter possible today?"

"That's right. I just started doing that instead of trying to be his happiness. That wasn't my job anyways, his joy and happiness needed to come from God, not me. I know he was juggling a hard process and I was there for him to talk to, but if he chose to keep it to himself that was okay. I would go to bed exhausted and still be tired in the morning but more refreshed I loved the verse about God's mercies are new every morning, it encouraged me and gave me hope for another day.

As the cancer continued to grow my heart was anxious about what the end of life would be like for your dad. When I looked too far into the future I had to reel it back in and look at today, and the manna of today and not worry about all the unknowns, for when I looked at the unknown future I would miss the gift that was in today. And as you know the days with your father were limited. Actually, the days with everyone are limited and we need to focus on the here and now. I remember it was such a hard thing to balance, staying in the present yet knowing, I had a future to plan for with you kids that didn't include your father and all of our finances were up in the air. Megan, I know, I understand. These were times of immense instability but the only thing that kept me stable and sane was my hope in the rock, Jesus the one who would never change.

Megan, sometimes it was a lonely place to be. Preparing to be a widow was such a surreal experience I mean how does one even prepare? It isn't something I had ever thought about or been taught anything about. My friends loved me the best they knew how but no one got it. No one else besides you kids ever saw your dad cry. No one else knew how painful it was to watch him struggle for breath or cough uncontrollably due to the cancer in his lungs. No one was there during the cold lonely nights preparing for his death. Megan, I never felt so helpless as I did watching him cry. He didn't like the fact he was leaving but yet he wouldn't prepare for leaving. Megan, you don't know how many times I asked him to write letters for you and your brothers for special moments in your life"

My heart was pounding faster now, "You did?" I asked thinking of how much those words from him would mean now.

"Yes, sweetie, I tried over and over until one day he asked me not to talk to him about it and I had to let it go. It wasn't that he didn't want to leave you words of advice it was just that he couldn't mentally get to a place that included thinking of not being there for all your big moments. It was just too heartbreaking for him. So that is why I always had my phone out recording videos and taking pictures of every single moment with him as I could. If he wouldn't make letters for you, I would do my best to preserve the memories of him."

"And you did an excellent job of that, look around," I said pointing to the walls covered with pictures that included my dad.

151

"Maddy who is that?" I said pointing to a picture of me on my dad's lap

near the end of his life.

"Papa," her little voice said.

My mom's eyes filled with tears. Yes, we had kept his memory alive.

"Mom it's a long story but I really believe he can see our good

moments, I believe he has seen my graduations, wedding day and the

day Maddy was born"

"Me too, I hold on to that belief and it makes it hurt less. Your father

was a great man who just didn't know how to handle what was

happening to him at the end of his life. I mean who really does? I pray

that I go quickly so I don't have time to ponder what life will be like

after I am gone."

"Mom, don't talk that way, I need you here with me!" I said not even

letting myself imagine what my life would be like without my mother

on earth. She was an angel sent by God to help me process my life with

paralyzed Ryan and help me process motherhood. I couldn't imagine

having gone through the past few years without her beside me to hold

me and cry with me and get through a life I never imagined.

"Your father loved us all so much and God answered his

prayer at the end, do you know what his prayer was Megan? His prayer

was that if he had to go, he wanted to not have the end where he wasn't able to take care of himself be long and drawn out. He always prided himself in taking care of himself and he didn't like asking for help. He didn't want to have someone bathe him and change him, although we would have happily done that for him. When it was his time, God took him quickly before his physical body got that bad. It was still extremely painful, but he didn't have to suffer anymore. He entered glory quickly. No more sorrows, no more pain. Can you imagine that Megan?"

"Yes," I replied, knowing that I could imagine heaven more than she had any idea. I longed to be back in the presence of Jesus and away from the pains of the world. I longed to be with my Daddy and my whole great cloud of witnesses. I knew that God's plan for me on earth was not over yet and I was put here to be the best that I could be at being Ryan's' wife and Maddy's mom. I wanted to do the best job I possibly could. I wanted the day I walked or flew into heaven, to hear the words "Well done my good and faithful servant" and with that, I resolved to be the best wife that I could be and never look back.

Chapter 20

I stayed busy taking care of Ryan and Maddy. Maddy was growing up before my eyes and was now five years old. Maddy was loving school and was learning to read. I loved helping her with homework and listening to her read. Often, I would sit with her as she read to Ryan. Over the years Ryan had remained in a positive place. Like all of us, he had his days. He had the times he cried a lot and yelled out in anger. There were times he talked about what it would be like to die and times he wouldn't even talk. Knowing how to be there for him was challenging. Sometimes he wanted to talk but most times he just wanted to be alone to process things on his own. I learned the dance and balance of how to best support him.

It was a typical Saturday and Maddy was up and running around at seven like it was a school day. That girl never seemed to slow down or even sleep in.

"Mommy, Mommy, today is a good day! It's Saturday! That's good but sometimes I do miss school, but I love being with you and daddy all day! Can I read to daddy today, pretty please?"

'Yes, Maddy bug, but we will have to wait for him to wake up first." I said as she jumped on my bed.

All Maddy had ever known was a paralyzed father. She didn't know any different, but she was beginning to show evidence that she was starting to be bothered by it. I recalled a conversation we had when she was four years old.

"Mommy, why can't daddy ever get up and play with me?" Although I had explained this to her, her entire life I patiently told her again. "Well Maddy, when you lived in my tummy your daddy was in a bad car accident. We were really scared, and we thought he might have died, but God saved him for us, He wanted him to be here for you, to be born and to grow up. When he was in the accident, he became paralyzed which means he wants to move his body but it won't work. He can only move his mouth. Maddy bug, he wants to play with you, He wishes he could play ponies and dress up and all kinds of things with you but he just can't but good thing he can still play I spy.

I thought about how the two of them loved looking at an item in the room and having the other person ask questions about it. It wasn't that hard to guess as Ryan's object was in whatever direction his head was facing and Maddy always picked things she was staring at too. It was the cutest thing to watch them play this game, they had formed a priceless bond in these times. The bonding started when Maddy was born, laying on Ryan's chest, when she got too heavy for that we made a chair that attached to the bed so Maddy could always be closer to her hero, her superman, her daddy. Sometimes as a mother, it broke my heart that she would never have a daddy to take her to father-daughter dance or walk her down the aisle, but at least he could be emotionally present even if he couldn't always be physically present. I myself had felt the pain of having an absent dad and I didn't want that for my baby.

"While we wait for daddy why don't you snuggle with me and we will watch cartoons"

"Yay, mommy!" Maddy said as I was pretty strict with screen time anytime She had the rare opportunity to watch tv she was very excited.

I listened to the sounds of the cartoon characters talking and gently stroked Maddy's back. There were few things greater in the world than Saturday morning cuddles with Maddy. What would life be like if I hadn't had Maddy? I don't even like to think about it. God's timing was so incredibly perfect with her. She was our ray of sunshine in our darkest times. I would be so lonely without my little angel. She had also given Ryan such joy and purpose. I was so thankful for the gift of her life. She looked a lot like Ryan. She had his brown hair, brown eyes, and deep dimples.

I closed my eyes and began to feel myself start to relax. Suddenly a sensation I hadn't felt in five years took over. The world started spinning and bright lights flashed in all directions. Wait, I thought this season was over, I thought I had made my decision, what was happening?

There I was again amidst an endless field of bright yellow tulips. "Why am I here?" I thought.

I saw a rainbow stretching high across the endless vibrant blue sky. The colors were more vivid than any I had ever experienced on earth before. I started walking forward through the tulips. Step after step I continued, turning in all directions looking for someone to talk to me. On all of my other trips, I had either heard a voice or seen people who had specific messages for me that were what I needed to hear. This time was different. I could sense it, I wondered what the purpose of this trip was, maybe it was just a dream, maybe all the trips were just dreams. Maybe healthy Ryan hadn't actually existed, maybe that was all part of a dream to show me what could have been. Sometimes my worlds were blurred when I entered this dimension.

I continued walking for what seemed like a long time but I didn't know how much time had passed. Although I must have walked for miles, I never grew tired or hungry or hot or cold. I always stayed at just the right temperature.

This place was unexplainable, I had never told anyone about it, I had kept it as a sacred secret between me and God. No one would understand not even Ryan. I also knew that no one would believe me. I took a deep breath in and felt the peace that I could only feel while in this place. I kept walking and suddenly as if out of nowhere a small stream appeared. It had the clearest blue water I had ever seen. As I approached it I saw the shape of someone who appeared to be wading in the water. As I walked closer his features became clearer to me. He was clothed in all white and a bright light shone over his face. I knew who he was, the kindness in his eyes was unmistakable. I fell to my knees in reverence and awe. Here I was again before my maker and creator.

"Hello, my daughter," he said as I stared at him again. I was awestruck by the peace that exuded from him and covered me. I got up and ran into his arms. I felt peace instantly cover my body.

"I am so glad you are here my Megan," he said with a twinkle in his eyes. I loved the way he called me my Megan, I felt so unworthy of his love. As I stepped back, I noticed the scars on his wrists. Somehow, I had not seen them before. I knew those scars were from when he died on a cross for me. I knew He did that selfless act so I could spend eternity with him. Many times in my life, it had been difficult for me to grasp just how much Jesus loved me. The time he showed me the tears in the bottle helped, but I still couldn't comprehend in my earthly mind how he could love me so much.

"I am glad to see you too Jesus," I said as I tried to take in who I was in front of.

"Megan, I am so proud of you and the way you have made the best of your life with Ryan. You have put his needs above your own and have kept your vows to love him in sickness and in health. I am so very proud of you. So very proud."

I was overtaken by the emotion of hearing him say that he was proud of me. On the endless nights of taking care of Ryan and Maddy and I felt no one saw or cared but it was nice to know that he did. He was there with me and for me, just like he had shown me before with the tears in a bottle. "Thank you," I said quietly, barely able to get the words out.

"Megan, you have been living with Ryan for five years now. You have been amazing. I love watching sweet Maddy grow, she really is a beautiful girl. She has her dad's smile. Megan, there are going to be more choices you will have to make. More roads you will have to decide which one to go down. I am glad that you understand that I don't cause pain, but I allow it. I always have an intricate plan of how all things will work out for my good for those who love me. You can rest in the fact that I always have a plan and always have your best interests in mind. This is not my original plan for the earth. Sin has changed things and has caused sickness and disease and all kinds of hard things.

I know you still pray every night for a miracle for your Ryan. I know you still pray that one day he will wake up and miraculously be able to walk. I love your persistence in never giving up on your prayer. I love that you always have hope. Without hope, life can be pretty bleak. You always keep the hope alive and help Ryan to keep the hope alive as well. I want you to know I hear every single prayer, even when I am silent and I don't do what you pray for. I still hear you. Your words are precious to me. You are teaching Maddy about me and that is one of the best things you can do.

"You are doing your best to make sure Maddy knows me and continues to stay close to me. Megs I know you have already been through so much with the death of your father, Ryan's accident and so much more but since you are still on earth, the storms are not over yet.

You are going to go through more storms but keep clinging to me and I will never let you drown, ever. Keep your eyes on me now and when the next storm hits, if you take your eyes off me it will be much harder to survive, but if you stay connected to me, spending time with me it will help you survive the storms of life.

Megan you have no idea how many people are watching you, observing how you handle storms and you have always done such a fabulous job of pointing them to me. Please keep pointing to me, I am using you to help countless lives. Sometimes I give you the gift of seeing who you are helping and the majority of the time you don't even have a clue of who the people are that you are helping. Megs there are a lot of them. Like I said I am so proud of you.

You have been faithful with a little and will continue to be faithful with a lot. There are more things coming so I want to make sure you are grounded in your faith, that your roots are deep and strong. The enemy will try to drown you. He is ruthless. He knows how valuable you are to me and how much good you are doing. He will try to take you, Ryan, and even sweet Maddy down. You have to be alert and on guard."

"Megan, I know you have suffered immensely. I know there are pains that only you know about. I know of several moments that no

161

one sees, the moments when it feels like dying would be easier than living, but Megan I want to show you something, let's take a walk sweet girl. He began walking along the stream and motioned for me to join him. The babbling brook was so beautiful and I could see shiny objects near the edge, shimmering diamonds seemed to materialize near the edge of the water and golden crowns and all kinds of objects made from gold seemed to just appear. My favorite color of blue jewels- aqua marine were all along the stream.

"Jesus, what are all these jewels? They are so beautiful!"

"Megan" he said as he picked some up a sparkly diamond bracelet,

"Can I have your arm?

"This is for you," he said as he clasped it around my wrist. It was the most dazzling bracelet I had ever seen. The diamonds seemed to sparkle brighter than any I had ever seen on earth, catching the light of Jesus and sparkling even brighter.

I was in total shock. How could Jesus be giving me such a beautiful gift? I didn't deserve this.

"Why, why is it for me?"

"Megan you are earning rewards for all you are doing. You have selflessly given up your needs and wants for your family and the good of me and my kingdom. These are just a preview of what is to come when you enter heaven at the end of your life."

I had never felt more like a princess in my whole life. On my wedding day, I felt special, but that was pale in comparison to this.

"Megan, you have earned all of this, he said as he pointed to the endless rows of jewels by the riverbank.

"I don't know what to say, I don't deserve this, I am a sinner."

"Yes, my daughter but you have been forgiven. It is all erased, all gone and you have done a lot of good on earth so far, and I still have more plans for you, I still have work I need you to do, but I wanted to give you the opportunity to see that you are earning rewards in heaven."

Overwhelmed by his love I stared into his kind eyes. Not only had he saved me from hell now he was giving me eternal rewards brighter than I had ever imagined.

"Thank you" were the only words that I managed to get out. Thank you didn't seem like a big enough word for the amount he had done for me. Not only had he blessed me with so many things on earth he was blessing me with things in heaven. I wanted to go home and shout it everywhere how amazing he is.

"Megan, I wanted to show you this today so that you know it does all matter. I see it all. The times when you get up in the middle of the night

163

to change Ryan's catheter or get up because Maddy had a nightmare. I see it all. I really do. Even when it seems like there is no one who will ever know all that you do, I see it and you are loved and will be rewarded. This is just a small representation of what is waiting for you. You are even more beautiful than this bracelet that I created for you. You are my first thought. I mean that, I want to give you a new name. Your name is no longer Megan, your name is My first thought. Megan, I know that you don't comprehend what that means, I know that you don't get it but please try. I think of you when I paint the sunrise and I think of you when I paint the sunset and everywhere in between. Do you know how much you love Maddy? Well, I love you that much times infinity! The depths of my love are too big for your human mind to comprehend. When you go back to your life and things get hard, and they will, please remember how much I love you and the depths of my love, please remember this bracelet and the other rewards you are earning. And one more thing Meg's, can I have this dance?"

With that, the sweetest music I had ever heard filled the air in all directions. It was the ultimate surround sound. Suddenly I was clothed in the most elegant gown I had ever seen. It was shiny white with sequins and a small diamond filled tiara was upon my head.

Slowly we danced to the sweetest music I had ever heard. Dancing felt like floating as we swayed to the music.

I was so blessed to get this supernatural experience with my savior. It was the most special thing I had ever experienced, and his love gave me comfort and peace to face whatever may come my way. I knew that returning to earth I was sure to encounter thousands of more trials, but I knew that God was growing me through every trial and ultimately, I would be here again and once again dance with my savior.

Chapter 21

As the music ended, I looked into the eyes of Jesus. I was still overwhelmed by his peace and love. His peace was unlike anything I had ever experienced. It wasn't like the kind of peace where you feel okay, but so much deeper. There were so many feelings and emotions that I had never experienced on earth before. In this place, it was as if all the good emotions were amplified and the bad ones were erased.

"Megan, I want you to be ready."

"Ready for what?" I replied wondering what he was talking about.

"I want you to be ready for another storm that is coming."

"Can you tell me what it is or when it is?"

"No, Megan that is part of how you build trust in me, by clinging to me every day as you don't get to know the future. Just keep trusting me no matter what. No matter what happens I am still in control and I still have a plan. Please get that. The enemy will try to make you think that I don't have a plan, but I promise you I do. I always have a plan my dear first thought, always"

I never wanted to leave his side. I didn't want to leave the peaceful bliss I was feeling and the experience of being with Jesus, but it looked as though my time was almost up. He seemed to be preparing me for something big.

"It is time to return to earth, my love."

And with those words lights flashed around me, and everything started moving. I opened my eyes and I was back in my warm bed snuggled up with Maddy, it was like no time had passed at all. It was like I had been dreaming, but I knew that it was so much more than a sweet dream. I knew I had visited heaven with Jesus. I kissed the top of Maddy's head and got up from the bed. I wanted to go check on Ryan. He was usually up by this time in the morning. adjusting back to this world I put one foot in front of the other and made my way down the hallway. I looked in on Ryan, he appeared to be peacefully sleeping but as I got closer, he opened his eyes.

I noticed that there was a lump starting to form on Ryan's wrist, at first I didn't think anything of it, of course, Ryan couldn't feel it so it didn't do any good to ask him about how he was feeling. One morning I went to check on Ryan as usual and I touched his wrist and felt the mass on his bone and knew it was not good. I knew it was time to call in Ryan's doctor. The next morning the doctor came over. I watched as he carefully inspected Ryan's wrist. I could tell by the look on his face that whatever he was thinking must not be good.

"Ryan, as hard as it is for us to take you into a medical office, you need to have a biopsy done on your wrist. There appears to be some kind of growth and we need to get it checked immediately. My heart sank with this news. For real? Was my husband really going through another health complication in addition to his already difficult paralyzation? This just seemed to be too much. I prayed that it would be a non-cancerous growth that could easily be removed.

The day of his biopsy arrived, and my stomach was in all kinds of knots. With the help of my mom we were able to load Ryan into our special handicap van that made it possible for Ryan to remain in his wheelchair strapped in while I drove to the hospital. Hospitals always made me nervous. From watching my father die to the trauma of Ryan's accident I did not have very many happy memories at hospitals, the only good thing that happened at the hospital was the birth of our little angel, our Maddy.

As I parked in the closest handicapped parking spot and got Ryan out of the car I wondered what the future would hold. Surely God wouldn't allow this growth to be cancer, right? We had already been through so much, suddenly the conversation I had with Jesus came quickly to mind. "Be ready for a storm" This must be the storm he was talking about. This storm seemed too big, too scary. As I wheeled Ryan into the hospital, he didn't say anything, He had become even more withdrawn and reserved recently. I didn't blame him, in his 31 years of life he had been through more than most people twice his age or even 3 times his age had been through.

We went to the pre op room and the nurses went to work taking his vitals and preparing him for his biopsy. Even though he couldn't feel anything they would still be putting him under anesthesia. Soon, it was time for him to be taken back to have his biopsy done. I watched them wheel him away and decided to wander the halls of the hospital. When I was a child this was like a game but now I did it for exercise.

I looked down at my smart watch and knew I needed to rack up more steps for the day. I walked at a quick pace down a long sterile hallway, I kept going and suddenly I saw a sign marked "chapel". The stain glass windows on the door looked so inviting, I loved the way the glass appeared in the sun. I decided to put my walk aside for a little while and see what the chapel was like. I felt immediate peace when I walked in. I heard the serene sound of a waterfall as I saw a small stream of water cascading over a rock and the peace of the sounds covered the entire room. I knew in an instant that the very breath of God was in the room.

It was that unmistakable feeling of peace I had when I would take my trips to heaven. It was as if a piece of heaven had been brought into this very room. I sat down on a bench near the cascading water. I closed my eyes and began to feel a prayer.

"Jesus, here we are again. Here I am again at a loss of knowing what the future will hold, a loss of knowing what is happening with my Ryan. God, I don't get it. First, he is paralyzed and now he might have cancer? It's just too much."

The tears were now freely flowing down my face, saltiness ran into my mouth and I began to lose my control and composure. I had found in all of the pain that the times I lost control of being all put together were the times I was the most vulnerable and the most open to hearing from God. When I became raw, open, and exposed then the healing began. As long as I covered myself with a protective layer I would never heal and move forward. As I continued crying from the depths of my broken heart I heard an audible voice.

"Megan, my love, I am collecting your tears, you are not alone and I do have a plan. Just cling to me."

Surprised I opened my eyes but there was no one around. Did I hear that right? Usually I heard from God in my head, but this time was different, this time was a distinct voice out loud. My God had really never left me, and he would really never forsake me. He was near me always and Forever. I stayed in the chapel for several more minutes. I wandered around the hospital for hours. Soon my pager buzzed indicating Ryan was done with the biopsy. I went back to his room and was met by the doctor.

"The biopsy went well; we got a pretty large chunk. We will let Ryan recover here for a few hours and then you can take him home. Unfortunately, the results of a biopsy take a long time so try to be patient and not worry as you wait on the results." That request was way harder than it sounded.

I took Ryan home that day and tried to forget about the possibility of cancer living in his body. Cancer was such a scary word to me. Cancer was something only other people had to deal with, I mean we were already dealing with permanent paralyzation who had ever heard of adding cancer on top of that? It was all too crazy for me to comprehend.

The days turned into weeks and finally about two weeks after the biopsy we got a call from the doctor.

"Can you put me on speaker so both of you can hear?"

I knew from that request and the tone of his voice that it must be bad news.

"Ryan, I am sorry to tell you that you have a very rare bone cancer, it is a kind of sarcoma.

My world started spinning, how could this be possible? How could my Ryan be paralyzed and have cancer? How could he be so unfortunate to actually have both of these life altering things happen to him?

"We would like to start you on chemotherapy right away. Given your paralysis this is going to be different than the usual protocol, you will be able to have chemotherapy at home. But, as you probably know chemotherapy will make you very sick along with a lot of other complications, I will send you all the information about. Ryan, this treatment will give you the best option of surviving as well as it not spreading. We also need to get you in asap for a CT scan to see if the cancer is anywhere else in your body, I am so sorry for this news I have to give you today, I wish It was better.

With those words I fell to the floor. All the strength I had been trying to keep dissipated under the weight of my body. I wanted to be strong for Ryan but I feared I had no more strength left anywhere inside of me. No more strength, just weakness. No more will to fight, to live

172

or to continue down the pain of life as I knew it. I suddenly had a strong urge to find all the pills in the house and take them at once. I wanted to end the pain. Heaving in and out trying to find just a small pocket of air, I felt a tiny hand upon my back and heard a tiny voice say "Mommy" and with that I was brought back to my reality that I did indeed have a lot to live for.

I was my Maddy's mother and Ryan's wife, there was no way I would leave them alone to deal with the future. I knew that thought was from the enemy and I would fight having it again. I was a warrior. A warrior for God. I had survived some of the most grueling times and yet I was still here. I had been bruised and scarred and left to die a few times, yet I never had, God wasn't done with me yet. I had a battle ahead of me but there was no way I would give in and give up now, no way. I was a fighter and I was ready to fight. Sure, sometimes I would get kicked around and feel weak but overall I was strong in my weakness because in my weakness He would become strong.

With God on my side there was absolutely no battle that I couldn't handle no army I couldn't go up against whether it was paralyzation, cancer or even death. I was ready and I would fight like the warrior I was to defeat the enemy and be the best version of me that I could be.

Chapter 22

Having cancer as part of our daily vocabulary took some getting used to. Back when I was a kid it was part of my daily life, but that seemed like an eternity ago. Soon after Ryan's biopsy he had a Pet scan. The scan was particularly difficult because Ryan was paralyzed, and it took extra people and support to keep him stable in the small tube he was put through to take a picture of his body. I remember when my dad used to have scans and how waiting for results used to feel like it took forever, we would wait on pins and needles to see if the cancer had grown or spread. Here I was again, but this time awaiting the results of Ryan's scans. How was it that I had to deal with cancer again, wasn't once in my life enough?

On a cold dark fall day, the doctor came to see us. This happened quite a lot as it was difficult for Ryan to go to the doctor's office. When the doctor arrived at our house, I could tell by the look on his face that his news couldn't be good. I had tried to prepare myself for the worst but there is only so much you can do to prepare for life-shattering news. He sat down beside Ryan and was at eye level with him.

"Ryan, I am afraid I don't have good news, I so wish I did. You and Megan have become like family to me. I am afraid I have to tell you that in addition to the cancer in your wrist it is also in your lungs and appears to be spreading to other organs. It is stage four cancer"

. Stage four cancer the words echoed in my mind over and over like a broken record. I knew from firsthand experience what stage four cancer was. I didn't need anyone to explain it to me. It was almost always a death sentence. I knew of a few people who had survived but for the most part people with stage four cancer didn't live too many more years after diagnosis. I knew how awful the last stages of life could be and I was even shielded as much as possible from it when I was a child. I looked at Ryan and he looked like he was numb to it all, numb to the pain of being paralyzed and numb to the reality of cancer.

For the moment I didn't let myself feel the intense pain of the reality in front of me. I had gotten good at dealing with what was right in front of me and then in my own time I let myself feel the pain of the situation in my own time and in my own ways.

"What do you suggest for his treatment doctor?" I said matter of factly. I knew I wouldn't like the answer, but I had to ask it.

175

"Well this is a very rare form of bone cancer and its very aggressive. We have several different routes of treatment that you can do, but none of them have been proven to work. They will make you very sick and we do not know if it would be effective. The first one involves getting treatment every day for five days. Normally it is done in the clinic, but we can most likely arrange to have it done here at your house.

"Can you tell us the name of the treatment so we can learn more about it before we decide?" I said.

He went on to say the complicated name of a treatment that was completely foreign to me. Ryan still hadn't said a word.

"Ryan, what are you thinking?" I said after the doctor had left.

"I am thinking this is not fair! Not only am I paralyzed I now have cancer that is spreading through my already worthless body. How do you think I feel?" He said in an accusatory tone.

There were so many times before this and I am sure there would be many to come when his tongue would pierce me with the fire of his angry words coming from the pain in his body, mind and heart.

Sometimes the things he spewed at me would be so toxic that I would shield myself with a layer so strong that it could not penetrate into my soul. If I listened to the words he spewed I could be curled up in a ball or hanging from a noose. It was a good thing that I had been strong from a young age and that I had already been a warrior facing

death since I was a child or his words might just get to me. I thanked

God for the experiences of my past to protect me from the present and

the future that was sure to come. God became my shield when the

words were thrown at me.

Thankfully, I never internalized them and was able to turn the

harsh words into opposites and quote the promises of God when he

spewed the lies of the enemy at me. For example when he called me

stupid I would say " I am fearfully and wonderfully made," knowing

who I was in Christ protected me from being damaged in the wake of

his pain.

I had learned it was best to leave Ryan alone when he got like

this. I used to try to talk to him, but I learned that only made things

worse. I learned to walk away and pray; it became a mantra I would say

and even something I had taught Maddy as she had been caught in the

path of his angry moments a few times.

"Walk away and pray Maddy, that is what is best to do" I

learned that when people were on lots of medications and in immense

amounts of pain the best things that I would do was to walk away.

Engaging in the conversation only added fuel to the fiery darts that

were pointed at me. I had learned from my counselor that the darts

177

were in fact him, not me. I learned that hurting people hurt people and I began to detach myself from feeling anything for him.

Ryan and I had a few conversations about what to do about treatment and we decided to try the first chemotherapy option given to us. The thought of being around chemo again made my stomach churn. I had spent too many days as a child seeing my father on chemotherapy and seeing him lose his hair and listening to the sound of him throwing up. I hated that my Maddy was also going to have to experience this pain. I could try shielding her from it all but it would find a way to her.

The day came to start Ryan's chemo and Maddy was at school. I had arranged for the treatments to all be done while she was at school, at least for now she wouldn't have to see him getting the treatment. As the nurses carefully hooked Ryan up with an IV I once again felt like this couldn't be real, but the chemo bag and beeping pump assured me that it was in fact reality. Pump after pump I heard the chemo being injected into his paralyzed body and prayed it would kill the cancer and he wouldn't get too sick. For five days in a row he was hooked up for about three hours each day to the drugs that we hoped would kill the cancer.

A few days after the first treatment, I saw pieces of Ryan's dark brown hair on his pillow and I knew he was starting to lose his hair. This was the part that stood out to me so much when I was a child, how I watched my daddy's once strong body turn frail and his hair began to fall out.

I looked at Ryan as I tried to hold back my tears.

"Ryan, would you like me to shave your head"

"Yes, let's do that"

I got the clippers and set about shaving his head. With every buzz I heard and piece of hair that fell to the ground my heart broke a little more. I remembered how I was supposed to consider everything pure joy, but shaving my paralyzed cancer ridden husbands head made it hard to see this as joy. How do you have joy when the very place that you stand on is shaking? When you feel like there is nowhere to balance yourself, how do you have joy then?

As soon as I finished Ryan said,

"Megs I don't feel good" I quickly brought him a plastic bag with a circle at the top which the nurses had given us for this very situation. I held the plastic circle to his mouth and watched helplessly as he threw up over and over until there was nothing left for his body to get rid of.

Holding water up to his mouth I thought This can't be worth it, this can't be worth it.

Our already almost impossible life had become unbearable. Ryan's quality of life was awful. He would wake up in the morning for what? To force a half smile at Maddy and then throw up for the rest of the day? It would be worth it if we knew it would work and kill the cancer, but now knowing was so hard. In addition to the nausea we also had to watch Ryan's temperature, for an even slightly elevated one could be deadly and many people who had cancer actually died from complications of their low immune systems from the treatment. The days were brutal and the nights even worse.

After a few months of treatment Ryan had his scans again to see if the cancer was growing or spreading, the hope that was because of the treatment it would be the same or a little smaller. I tried to keep busy while we waited for results so I wouldn't drive myself crazy thinking about what the results could be.

Then the day came that the phone rang. Once again, the doctor asked to be put on speaker phone and once again my heart dropped while hearing the tone in his voice.

"Megan and Ryan, I am sorry to tell you that the tumors have all grown and have now spread to your lymph nodes and lungs. The treatment is not working.

"Really?" I wanted to scream over the phone.

"I think it is time you decide if you want to continue treatment, many people at your stage stop and focus more on quality of life and just make the most of the time they have left."

The time they have left...the words rang over and over in my head, the time they have left. Could this really be happening, could my husband really be dying? Did I really have to go through this twice in my life? Did my sweet Maddy really have to deal with this? I couldn't imagine the thought of her losing her daddy. Although he had never been able to participate in many things with her at least he had always been there for her at our house every day. He had been a constant in her life, how could I consider the death of my daughter's dad to be pure joy? I thought I could consider all things pure joy, but this? This was way too much for anyone to consider pure joy, and with that I felt my joy once again come under the crippling effect of paralyzation.

Chapter 23

After the doctor left, Ryan and I were alone to talk about the options.

"What are you thinking Ryan?" I said and let the uncomfortable silence fill the air. I knew he needed time to process things in his own way which was usually alone and with a lot of time. Ryan was never one to make quick decisions which was pretty opposite of my impulsive full of feelings decisions.

"I don't know Megan, there really isn't a good choice. Either I continue with treatment and keep fighting it or I just give up. I don't want people to think that I have given up!"

"Ryan, deciding to stop treatment is not giving up. It is simply picking a different route. It is not like game over and giving up in a game. I still believe that God can heal you. We just know that the treatments are making you super sick and aren't helping to shrink the tumors and the cancer is still spreading. I support you either way, there are valid reasons for both choices."

I watched the tears now flowing freely down his face.

"Megan I am just so tired of being so sick. I want to enjoy life more; I don't want to be sick every time Maddy comes home from school. I want to be able to talk to her hear about her day, listening to her read and all the things I used to do with her.'

"I get that Ryan, and that is why it sounds like you know what you should do. You should stop treatments and we can focus on your quality of life. You can live without feeling sick every moment and giving hours and hours to chemotherapy each week. Ryan, I think it is a good choice and please don't worry for even one second that people will think you are giving up. First of all, you aren't giving up and second of all, it doesn't matter what anyone else thinks. If you think it is the right decision, then it is."

After that conversation, I called the doctor and told him we were not going to do anymore treatments. It made me sad to realize there were not anymore options for Ryan but knew that it was the best decision for him. I had never thought of a timeline for Ryan, in fact I had never wanted to know but when I called the doctor something inside me made me want to ask him.

"Dr. Woods, I have never asked this because I haven't wanted to know, but I feel like now I want to mentally prepare and know how to prepare Maddy. How long do you think Ryan has to live?"

My heart beat faster and faster as I waited. I expected the answer to be two to three years.

"Well Megan, it is hard to say but based on the type of cancer he has and how fast it is growing I would estimate three to six months"

Silence was all I heard as I tried hard to comprehend the words that had just been spoken to me. As if someone had ripped holes in the vision of my future, I took a deep breath. I calculated in my head what months that could mean that I would lose my husband. I began crying and tried to muffle the tears, but it was too late. I knew the doctor felt bad as he tried to back pedal from the bomb he had just dropped on me.

"Megan that is only from what I have seen from others and it doesn't mean it will happen, each person and cancer is so different'.
"I appreciate you telling me, I needed to know, thank you, goodbye"
I knew I had to hang up before I completely lost control of my emotions. As I pressed the end button the weight of all the emotions I had been holding back cascaded from the dam of bottled up sorrow and pain. I slid to the floor and let all the tears come out. I began heaving uncontrollably and I felt like this had to be some kind of nightmare. How could God allow Ryan to live through his accident only to later die from cancer? The problems and thoughts were bigger than me.

I heaved and cried as I felt a mixture of tears and wet on the cold floor beneath my cheek. I cried until there was absolutely nothing left for me to cry. There were not words deep enough for the pain that invaded my very soul. The thought of Ryan no longer being with us was so foreign and hard to understand.

"God" I prayed aloud, "please heal my Ryan here on earth and please give me strength to endure what is coming. Please protect my sweet Maddy from the impact this is bound to have on her little heart." I knew Maddy was too young to understand the concept of death and I didn't even want to mention death until we knew it was a close and definite reality.

I tried to pull myself together as I knew Maddy would soon be getting off the bus and arriving home from school. I needed to put on a strong face for her.

Sure, the accident had changed Ryan and there were many activities that he already didn't participate with me in but at least he was always there. Strong and steady I could always count on Ryan being there for me in his room to talk to me and listen to me every single day. I could not even picture life without him. But I would have to start picturing life without him. It was a hard balance between staying in the day and not worrying and also planning for the future. I remember when my mom had talked about anticipatory grief, how she had explained that it is like a train is coming and there is nothing you can do to stop it when you know someone you love is about to die.

The hardest for me was knowing the train was headed for my little Maddy and there was nothing I could do to stop it. I knew the pain of losing a father and I didn't want her to have to experience the same depth of pain that I had, but what could I do to stop it? Absolutely nothing.

How could I make a decision about any future events when I didn't know how much longer Ryan would be alive? I had already been experiencing a new kind of guilt any time I was away from him, I felt guilty because now I knew his time was limited, now I knew the amount of times I would see him his bed resting was limited. Everything in my life hinged on how long Ryan would live. It was such a surreal place to be. Knowing I would soon be saying goodbye to the one I had loved my whole married life with was such a strange place to be.

My thoughts were interrupted but the sounds of Maddy opening the door. "Mommy" she yelled as she ran into my arms. Her excitement to see me every day after school never ceased to amaze me. "How was school today?"

"Great, I moved up a level in reading and got cupcakes to celebrate Lilly's birthday."

I loved how the simplest things brought joy to Maddy Joy. I want to have that simple childlike faith back as I watched her hang up her backpack and head to her designated snack drawer to pull out an after-school snack.

Watching her bouncing curls and wide-eyed smile how could I ever tell her that her hero, her daddy was dying? How could I ever say those words to her? Today wasn't the day and I would pray that God would give me the words to say and the timing to say them in.

After grabbing a snack, I knew exactly what Maddy would do, she ran to Ryan's room, jumped up on the chair and kissed his face.

"Hi Daddy, I love you, can I read to you? I even moved up a level!"

That's great honey," Ryan said with a smile on his face,

"Please read to me, it's one of my favorite parts of the day." Maddy grabbed a book, sat down and started to sound out words in her best reading try.

I wanted to etch this picture in my memory for all time. I knew just like everything else with Ryan our times for Maddy reading to her daddy were in fact limited. I took out my phone, snapped a quick picture and tried to soak in every detail I could. I knew from this day forward it would be one moment after another of creating and recording precious memories of moments I didn't want us to forget these times. I wanted Maddy to keep forever and it was my job to help record them for the days when she would no longer be able to recall the sound of his voice or the look of his face.

Chapter 24

Waking up to the reality that my paralyzed husband now had stage four cancer was almost too much for me to take. It reminded me of the early days of when Ryan was paralyzed. I would forget the horror of my reality while I was asleep and as soon as I would wake up I had a few seconds of peace and then bam the reality would hit me and all I wanted to do was go back to the peace of my dream world.

That is what it began to be like every morning but times a million. The only thing that got me out of bed was Maddy. Maddy was my driving force for making myself get out of bed. Maddy was the reason I could push through almost anything.

Christmas season was fast approaching, and it was all so bittersweet. Ryan's absolute favorite time of the year had always been Christmas. Knowing that this year could very well be his last Christmas season shook me to my already fragile core.

Ryan had always been a fan of Christmas lights, getting our tree the day after Thanksgiving and year-round Christmas music. We often started watching Christmas movies before Halloween even happened. I had always loved Christmas but had a new infusion of love for it since marrying Ryan. Maddy loved it as much as Ryan if not more. Her sweet little five-year-old self thought it was the best thing ever.

Maddy knew that Ryan was sick, but she didn't comprehend the full gravity of the situation and the possibility of his upcoming death. I didn't think she was ready for that truth until the day was closer. Five-year old's do not have a good grasp on time so I was afraid it would confuse her mind even more to mention anything about Ryan's death until it was imminent.

One night while I was tucking Maddy into bed with our usual nighttime rituals she surprised me with the depth of her questioning.

"Mommy, why doesn't God heal Daddy?" I stood stunned by her question not knowing quite how to answer. *God, give me the wisdom to answer my child,* I quickly prayed.

"Maddy, that is a good question, one that grown-ups don't even know how to answer. We know that God has the power to heal Daddy and we know he can. Sometimes God answers how we want and sometimes we don't get the answer we want and it's confusing. I want you to think about when we put together that big five-hundred-piece puzzle of the Christmas village, do you remember that?"

Eyes wide and paying full attention Maddy nodded "yes"

"Well Maddy, before the puzzle was put together it just looked like a bunch of random pieces, we couldn't yet see what it would make. Our lives are like pieces of a puzzle, we see only the pieces, but God knows what the whole puzzle looks like when it's completed. He pieces our lives together with other lives and things we don't understand to make a beautiful puzzle that we don't yet see. He may heal daddy and we will pray for that every day, but his puzzle piece may include healing him in heaven instead of earth and we have to trust that God in all his strength, wisdom and power knows how the puzzle will go together the best. Maddy continued to look at me "That makes sense Mommy. I just hope that the puzzle God is creating includes daddy's cancer going away on earth."

"Me too Maddy, me too" I said stroking her hair softly.

Did I believe the words I was saying to Maddy? Did I believe that God really knew best? In theory it was easy to believe. Let go and let God as the cheesy saying went. But did I really believe what I was telling my daughter? Did I really believe that God knew how to make the puzzle of my life? So many times I had tried to force the puzzle pieces into places I was sure they needed to go only to later see that it wasn't even close to right, but each time God in all his wisdom, grace

191

and mercy would pick up my pieces and slowly and lovingly place them back in the correct places.

That's the thing about God, he would never force his pieces into place, he would let me make my mistakes and always be there to mend them back together.

Kissing Maddy goodnight I turned off her light and walked towards Ryan's room.

I peered into the room and I could see little pieces of hair beginning to grow on his head as he had now stopped treatment. His nausea had lessened, and he was feeling better physically, but mentally he had been all over the place. As I stared at him, I recalled a conversation from earlier in the day.

"Ryan, I was thinking maybe you would want to write a letter or make a video or something for Maddy to have in the future."

Ryan glared at me.

"Why are you asking me to do that?" he said defensively.

"Because you may not be there at her special events like graduation and her wedding day and I want her to hear from you on those days. I think it would be really special for her."

"Why do you keep asking me? That would require me to go to a dark place and I am not ready for that" Ryan said as tears slipped down his cheeks. It was so hard to know how to talk to him these days.

In the beginning of our marriage I barely saw him cry and now he cried every day, every single day. I had tried many times to put myself in his shoes and to me the hardest part would be leaving Maddy. I would start to imagine her growing up without me and it was too painful, and I had to stop. Letting myself go there emotionally helped me to understand why Ryan had a hard time with leaving something for her. On the other hand, I thought about if I was not sure if I was going to be there for her all the things I would want to say to her, to tell her how much I loved her.

All the advice I would want to give all the life lessons I would want to leave her and it made me want to leave her a legacy behind. But Ryan and I were different and I had to let it go, this was not my gift to give and if he didn't want to leave special notes or videos behind I couldn't make him.

Ryan woke up and could sense my presence.

'Hey Megs,what's up?

"Just coming to check on you, I just put Maddy down for bed. She had some more questions about healing and God and all of this"

193

"What did you tell her?" He replied quickly.

"I told her the puzzle story again" I knew Ryan was familiar with the puzzle explanation of God as we had talked about it many times.

"Oh, I wish God would make my puzzle the way I want!" he said

"I know sweetie, this isn't the puzzle that any of us imagined when we got married, but it is our puzzle just the same"

"I know I just wish I had a different life, Megan do you remember how healthy I used to be?"

I recalled the stories he told me about his youthful days of playing baseball all growing up and I remembered when he was a college athlete playing baseball.

"Yes, I remember"

"Well those days are long gone; I can barely remember them" he said with a new level of sadness showing in his eyes.

"I do not understand God, why did he do this to me?" he said with a rage in his tone.

"Sweetie, I know it doesn't feel like it, but God did not do this to you. He allowed it, remember if God allowed it, I can accept it. I don't get it either, it doesn't seem fair to me either, but this is the way it is. I love you and I am sorry." I said as I stroked his face calmly.

"I hate this Megan, I don't want to leave you and Maddy, I know I am headed for eternal glory but how can it be so glorious without you two?"

Recalling my trips to heaven I had never told anyone about I decided to share a little with him without explaining it all.

"Ryan, it's hard to explain but you won't miss us when you are there. You will have a new level of peace than you have ever experienced before. There will be beauty and joy and indescribable peace. You will be able to run and jump and have no more pain. You will have a body that is even better than you had in your youthful days on earth. I know it is way too hard for our earthly minds to comprehend but I promise you won't miss us and then we will be there with you eventually. I know death is scary, but you have nothing to fear as you know where you are going."

"Thanks Megs" he said as somehow the words I had said began to calm him down. I was so thankful for my experience in heaven to be able to share with Ryan, maybe part of it was so I could help his transition into heaven even easier. For the first time I thought about Ryan and my daddy together in heaven, the thought immediately brought tears into my eyes as I thought of the two men I loved most together in eternal bliss. I couldn't wait to join them. I knew what would happen in the coming months would be the most painful thing I had ever experienced but the thought of where I was going and what I would experience always got me through.

Sometimes we can't avoid the fiery trials that we have to go through to refine us into the gold that God wants to create in us. I had been through plenty of fires before, but none could prepare me for the fire of death that was most definitely headed my way. There was absolutely nothing I could do to change it and I knew that it was going to hurt worse than anything else I had ever experienced.

Chapter 25

With each passing day, Ryan became weaker. As the cancer grew his body began to shut down. The tumor was so large in his lungs that you could see it protruding from his back on the back of his lungs. His coughing had increased and whenever I would hear the straining of his coughs it would remind me again of how sick he was. Living each day watching him deteriorate was something so emotional and deep I couldn't even put it into words. Loving someone so deeply that you know is about to leave is excruciating. Through the pain, I was reminded of the quote that says "Tis better to have loved and lost than never to have loved at all". I never truly understood those words until my Ryan was dying. I never understood how it would be to lose the very thing I loved the most.

To know each day that it may be the last was a mind shift. I had to balance between being present in the moment but also knowing the future was coming. Such a limbo kind of place to live.

Ryan was no longer getting enough oxygen on his own, so he required an oxygen tank most of the time. He also had had a PICC line installed while he was still able to leave the house so his pain medicine could easily be administered. He was on so much pain medicine that sometimes he didn't make sense. Sometimes he was confused, and he often would forget things we had already discussed. I had tried to talk to Maddy about Ryan dying, but it was so hard for her little mind to comprehend. I recalled a recent conversation Maddy and I had a few days ago.

Maddy and I sat on the floor of her room surrounded by dolls and stuffed animals in every direction. This was one of her favorite things to do, to sit in her make-believe world surrounded by her little playmates. I realized that this moment might be the perfect opportunity to talk to her about Ryan in a way that would make sense to her.

"Maddy, let's play pretend with the stuffed animals. Let's pretend this is daddy", I said while taking a golden lion with a big mane in my right hand, "and this I said taking a giant sheep is God."

Maddy giggled as I continued.

"This is you sweet girl" I said taking a brown pony with a spot on its hind quarters. I said handing the pony to her.

Taking the sheep in my hands I said in a low voice

"Daddy, I know you haven't been feeling well for a long time, you have been paralyzed for years and now you have cancer. I love you so much that I am going to bring you home to heaven to live with me forever. You won't have any more pain and you will be able to run and jump and play."

Taking the lion in the other hand I said in my best Ryan voice

"I'm not sure I am ready to go and it seems kind of scary to die, what will it be like?"

Maddy interrupted with her pony in hand.

"It's okay Daddy, I will be by your side and hold your hand when you have to go. Jesus will take good care of you"

I sat stunned by the maturity she showed as we played.

Taking the sheep again in my hand I said" That's right Maddy, you can be with your daddy to help him be brave. And Daddy, it isn't scary coming to live in heaven and I know you may not want to leave or feel ready to leave but I promise I will take care of Maddy and Mommy for you" I said in my best God voice trying to hold back the tears welling in my eyes.

"It's okay daddy," Maddy said stroking the lion with the pony. I studied her face as she spoke. Her maturity flowing way past her five years on earth. It was like God had been preparing her for this time. I was the one who seemed more scared than her.

"Thanks, Maddy, I love you so much" I said as the lion daddy.

199

"You're welcome Daddy" she replied.

"Maddy", I said, putting down the stuffed animals. "Do you understand that it's not just pretend that Daddy is dying but that he is actually dying?"

"Yes, mommy, I have heard you talk about it before."

"I am sorry you have to go through this my sweet girl" I said while pulling her onto my lap.

"But you want to know something good?" I said

"Yes mommy."

"Your daddy will be with my daddy! How cool is that?"

"Really, I never thought of that before, maybe they will play together?"

"I am sure they will. My daddy loved playing baseball and sports just like your daddy and I am sure they will love playing together."

"You think there is baseball in heaven mommy?"

"Oh yes, and all the things we love. God says it is even better than we can even imagine, and the best thing is that there are no more tears and no more pain there!"

"Wow, but what if you fall down and get hurt?" Maddy asked inquisitively.

"Well that's the really cool thing, you can't get hurt, I know Maddy all of this is hard for our minds to comprehend, we just have to trust God

200

about how amazing it is. Remember last summer when you asked Jesus to forgive your sins and come live in your heart? Well that very moment God says that he wrote your name in the Lambs book of life which means you have a place in heaven, daddy's name and my name are in it too and that means that even though daddy will go to heaven first, we will all be together again one day."

"I like thinking that mommy."

"Yes, it does make saying goodbye easier, knowing that it is only temporary," I said as I kissed the top of Maddy's head.

These were such adult concepts that I couldn't believe Maddy was able to comprehend what we were talking about.

"Maddy we don't know for sure when daddy will go to heaven or what it will be like, but we do know that God will be with us and help us through every step of the way. Sometimes it might look scary and sometimes I might have you go stay with Grandma."

"No! I want to be with Daddy when he goes to heaven" Maddy said emphatically as she interrupted me.

"Okay sweetie, we will just take it one day at a time and see what things are like. We are a family and if you are old enough to understand it, you can be with us"

"As for right now let's carpe' diem" I said as I tickled her sides.

201

"Yes, mommy lets seize the day!"

Maddy had known from a young age what those words meant. Each and every second we had with Ryan was a carpe diem moment even if in those times it didn't feel like it. Sometimes in the darkest of times when Ryan was sick beyond comprehension, I would wish those carpe diem moments away and immediately regret it. I knew in my heart that someday I would wish for those moments with him again. I knew that I never wanted to take any time together for granted.

With the words "Carpe' Diem" Maddy ran out the door and into Ryan's room. The bed had propped him up into a sitting position and his eyes fluttered open with the sound of Maddy approaching.

"Hi Baby Girl" he said in a quiet and weak voice.

"Hi Daddy" Maddy said as she leaned up to kiss his cheek.

"Can we watch a Christmas movie together?"

There were not many activities that Ryan could join us in but watching movies especially Christmas movies was a family favorite. I looked around the room at the string of lights I had put up along with a mini christmas tree.

"Yes, sweetie, how about Elf, I love that one and I need some laughs tonight"

"Yay, I 'll go get it" Maddy said running out of the room.

"And I will make cookies" I said going to turn on the oven. Nothing made us feel like a family more than a Christmas movie and fresh-baked chocolate chip cookies. For the duration of a movie we could tune out the world, tune into each other and forget a world that include pain medicine, oxygen machines and cancer. For a few hours, the three of us could just be. There was no worry about the future, no regrets of the past, just pure joy living and being in the moment together. Forgetting the fears of the unknown future we would get lost in another world. A christmas world with multiple laughs. Walking towards the kitchen I prayed

"Thank you God for the gift of this family. I may not have them forever, but I have them for today. I may not know what tomorrow holds but this moment we have each other and there is no greater gift I could ask for at this moment. Please give me the wisdom to know how to be the wife I need to be with Ryan, please help me know how to help him when he is crying and emotional and please help me to know how to lead my little Maddy down this valley of the shadow of death. Guide me as I guide her. Please give me the supernatural strength to do what I know is in front of me. Lead me please, lead me when I am alone and scared and I can't see my hand in front of my face. Lead me through the inevitable trials that I must walk through and make me into the woman you have created me to be. Thank you for creating me to be Ryan's wife and sweet Maddy's mom"

Entering Ryan's room to the sound of Christmas music on the tv I was covered once again with the peace that passes all understanding and I knew that once again, my God who had never failed me yet would indeed lead me through the most difficult time in my life and never ever leave my side, no matter what.

Chapter 26

The day I was fearing since I heard the word cancer was fast approaching. I had read books, searched internet sites, and spent countless hours talking to friends and the hospice nurse about what to expect when Ryan's death was near. There were signs and by the loss of appetite combined by the fact that Ryan could no longer stand up that the time was drawing near.

For months I had felt the same way I felt when I was expecting my first child, knowing the day was approaching but I couldn't do anything about it. Knowing the baby inside me was growing was the same, but opposite of how I felt about the approach of Ryan's death. I knew it was coming and I couldn't stop it, but unlike the joy that comes with birth I would experience the opposite with death, but on the other hand, Ryan would be experiencing joy. If I really loved him like I said I did I would release him to be out of pain and sorrow. I would release him from his cancer-ridden body and into his glorious body that was better than we could imagine.

Watching Ryan lose to death was too much for my human mind to comprehend. I felt like the whole world was spinning with people making their holiday plans and going to their parties and all I wanted for Christmas was to have one more Christmas morning with my complete little family. I was praying that Ryan would also make it to the new year but if I could only have one, I would pick Christmas.

Ryan was less coherent and awake every day. I found the moments with him were becoming rarer and even more precious. I knew our conversations were limited and I tried to be purposeful with every one of them. No longer were the days endless conversations dreaming about the future but more about recording every precious word that came out of Ryan's mouth. I wanted to have as many memories to leave Maddy with as possible.

A few days after Christmas Ryan opened his eyes and he looked at me and in a barely recognizable voice he said

"Megs I'm ready to leave something for Maddy for her wedding day." My eyes instantly filled with tears as I had long since given up the dream of him leaving something for Maddy and had dropped the subject when he said he couldn't.

"Okay sweetie, let me get a pen and paper"

I grabbed some nearby paper and pulled a pen out of my purse.

"I'm ready" I quickly wanted to get it all down before he ran out of energy.

"Dear Maddy" Ryan softly said as I wrote

"My precious baby girl, I want you to know I am so very proud of you. I wish I could be there with you today, please know I'm smiling down on you from heaven" Ryan said through tears. Suddenly the letter was even more emotional for me remembering how my dad wasn't there for me on my wedding day but how he told me he was watching from heaven.

He continued "I know whoever you have chosen to marry must be a very special man. I know you would only choose the best. I wish I could be there to walk you down the aisle" I wiped more tears from my eyes.

"But I know you have chosen someone else very special in your life to fulfill that role" I tried to imagine who that might be, maybe one of my brothers.

"Maddy my princess I wish I could be there to see how beautiful you are and what an angel you look like, but God called me home. I pray that you and your husband know Jesus as your savior and that you are working towards a triangle, something your mom and I learned a long time ago. What it means is you and your husband must both have a relationship with God and then have one together. That is the only way to succeed in a marriage. Sweetie, I'm proud of you for who you are. I don't even have to see you now to know you have accomplished great things. You are a beautiful girl and I know you will be a beautiful wife and one day a wonderful mother, just like your mom. You will go far in life and as sad as I am that I will not be able to be there, I know that i know, that I know that God will take care of you. Maddy, I know there are not enough words to make up for me not being there and like your mom tried to explain to you about the puzzle, we don't know all the pieces Maddy, we don't know why I had to leave you but we trust in something greater. We trust in the creator of the universe that he does have a plan and that he will make beauty out of ashes. I trust that when you think of me you can already see the ways he has turned your mourning into dancing, that you can see beauty in all directions. Maddy my love, I want you to have something special from me for this day. I want you to have this special bracelet as your something old and as a reminder of how much I love you my dear princess."

Ryan paused, "Megan will you open my top drawer, I ordered a bracelet online for Maddy before I was this sick. Can you get it for me?"

Opening his drawer I saw a tiny light blue box and instantly recognized it as Tiffany's. I brought the box to him and opened it up. Inside a tiny sachet bag was a silver linked bracelet with a heart on it. Engraved in tiny elegant letters it said "Maddy, I love you forever" and on the other side it said "xoxo Daddy" Tears began to fall down my face as I realized the significance of this precious gift.

"Ryan, it is beautiful, she will cherish it forever." I said as I envisioned the bittersweet day that Maddy would receive this priceless gift.

"Let me finish the letter" Ryan said. "I am sending love from heaven, I pray that today is everything you ever dreamed of and more, I love you always and forever, Love, Daddy"

"It's perfect Ryan, I will keep it safe and give it to her on her wedding day. I took the letter and bracelet and locked them away in my fireproof safe. Returning to the room, his eyes were now closed. His breathing began to rattle, and he showed more signs of death. I knew it was time to call the hospice nurse to check in with how he was doing.

When the nurse arrived, she looked Ryan over and said "It could be anytime now" I quickly called my mom and asked her to bring Maddy home from visiting her. When Maddy arrived, I talked to her before she entered Ryan's room.

"Maddy you know how we talked about Daddy going to heaven?" She nodded with wide eyes.

"Maddy, we think it might be time'"

Maddy's eyes instantly filled with tears and she said "No, I'm not ready yet"

"I know sweetie I don't know if I am either, but we don't have a choice. Let's go talk to him."

Holding Maddy's hand we walked towards Ryan.

"Hi Daddy" Maddy said as she kissed his cheek.

Ryan's eyes fluttered open. "Hi Sweetie, it's time for me to go to heaven now, I want you to know it's okay, your mom will take good care of you and I will always be watching over you"

Maddy soaked in every word "I know Daddy, it's okay that you need to go be with Jesus, I will be okay, I promise."

Ryan opened his eyes and looked at me.

"Megs thank you for loving me through it all. Thank you for staying by my side while I was paralyzed and when I got cancer. You gave up your life to take care of mine and I am so thankful for you. I love you"

"I love you too Ryan, it's okay that you need to go"

With those parting words Ryan closed his eyes for a final time, took his last breath and left his earthly body.

The silence that entered the room at the moment Ryan's soul entered heaven was unlike anything I had ever experienced before. The loss of a soul is an unexplainable experience. I looked at the shell of the man that once held my husband and was filled with both peace and sorrow in the same instant.

"He's gone Maddy" I said as we embraced in a hug. I let my baby cry for as long as she needed. While she was crying the room suddenly began to spin and flashes of light were everywhere, and I knew what was happening.

The spinning stopped and I opened my eyes and I was surrounded by bright yellow tulips in every direction Though it had been a while since my last visit I instantly knew where I was.

"Heaven" I whispered.

Suddenly to my right appeared a bright light that covered a man and I knew it was Jesus.

"Megan, my child, I brought you here to experience this moment" He said while pointing in front of him.

In the distance I saw my daddy once again, he appeared in the field when suddenly I saw Ryan walking towards him. No longer was Ryan paralyzed and I knew there wasn't a trace of cancer in his body. I watched my father open his arms and say "Ryan. welcome!" As if my father had always known Ryan, he embraced him in a hug as long lost family does. I was overwhelmed with joy seeing the two men I loved more than anything together. Not only were they together, but they were together in healthy bodies.

Jesus continued "I wanted to give you a glimpse into what is happening here with the men you love. I know on earth you have and will continue to experience the pain of missing them, but they are well, no longer in pain and they are together! Megan, I believe you chose right when you chose to continue with paralyzed Ryan. It by no means has been an easy life, but it has been an impactful life. Your life with Ryan has as you know touched so many more people than you can comprehend. And your impact is far from over.

Your work is not done. I have more lives for you to touch, more people for you to love and the impact that all of this will have on Maddy's life and those that Maddy comes into contact is more than your human mind can comprehend. I have given you the gift of visiting heaven in order to help you see what most people never see, how their lives impact others and how trials help them to become the best version of themselves. Maddy I love you, now it is time to continue your work on earth."

With that the world started spinning and I was back in the embrace of Maddy. I looked at Ryan's body that no longer contained his soul and thanked the Lord for the gifts he had given me and that through the trials I no longer had paralyzed joy.

The End

About the Author

Michelle Bader lives in Vancouver, WA with her three kids Hayden,

Hayley, and Payton. Her husband Luke recently moved to heaven after

a 16-year battle with cancer. She wrote a book about their cancer battle

in the book "Cancer Can't Crush Us" which can be found here.

Or you can search for it on Amazon. She hopes her books encourage

and inspire those going through hard times. She also has a podcast

called "The Peace Cast" that can be found on Apple podcast, Spotify

and anywhere you listen to podcasts. You can email her at

michellepbader@gmail.com

Follow her on IG @michellebaderauthor

Acknowledgements

Thank you to Kathy Johnston for helping me edit this book and encouraging me on my writing adventure. Thank you to my girl's night girls- Kathryn King-Ower, Melissa Schneider, Jill Deishl, and Melissa Sutton for listening to sample chapters and encouraging me to keep going even through all the discouraging feedback I was getting. You never let me give up on my dream!

Thank you to Deborah Johnston who provided real life experiences to base a Ryan's paralyzation on. I really appreciate your help, love and encouragement!

Thank you to my parents Steve and Karen Rommel who have ALWAYS supported me in all my many endeavors. You love and support me unconditionally.

Thank you to my kids who always believe in me and the goals and dreams I set out to complete.

Thank you to my amazing husband Luke in heaven, I am so thankful for all of your support and love over the years. I am so blessed that I was your wife for almost 17 years and although I miss you more than words can explain I love that you are healthy and having the best time in heaven!

Thank you, Jesus, for saving me and filling my life with indescribable peace. Without you my writing would be empty and meaningless, thank you for the promise of eternal glory!

Made in the USA
Coppell, TX
03 September 2020

36374625R00132